"You little witch," he said hoarsely

"A witch?" Kelly gave an indignant laugh and shook her head. "No, Byron. You can't blame me for how you feel. I didn't *make* you fall for me. And I didn't exactly ask to fall in love with you, either." She paused. "But I am willing to give up my home, my country—everything—to be with you."

Byron said with bitter irony, "You're very brave, Kelly. But—" He broke off and turned away. "It wouldn't work. There are too many differences between us, just as there were w—"

"With Elaine," Kelly supplied. "Go ahead, say it. Saying her name can't hurt me." She sighed, and said under her breath, "Heaven knows, she's alive enough in this house...."

SALLY WENTWORTH began her publishing career at a Fleet Street newspaper in London, where she thrived in the hectic atmosphere. After her marriage, she and her husband moved to rural Hertfordshire, where Sally had been raised. Although she worked for the publisher of a group of magazines, the day soon came when her own writing claimed her energy and time.

Books by Sally Wentworth

Don't miss any of our special offers. Write to us at the following address for information on our newest releases.

Harlequin Reader Service
901 Fuhrmann Blvd., P.O. Box 1397, Buffalo, NY 14240
Canadian address: P.O. Box 603,
Fort Erie, Ont. L2A 5X3

SALLY WENTWORTH

strange encounter

Harlequin Books

TORONTO • NEW YORK • LONDON
AMSTERDAM • PARIS • SYDNEY • HAMBURG
STOCKHOLM • ATHENS • TOKYO • MILAN

Harlequin Presents first edition January 1990
ISBN 0-373-11237-8

Original hardcover edition published in 1989
by Mills & Boon Limited

CHAPTER ONE

KELLY BAXTER was alone in the apartment, sitting at the desk by the window with a rapidly filling wastepaper basket beside her as she determinedly sorted through her parents' papers. The flat was warm, but when she glanced up at the double-glazed window she saw that the snow was falling again, thick flakes that covered still icy pavements even though it was now almost March. For a moment Kelly glowered at the snow, hating it, and blaming it for the car crash that had killed her parents on the way home from a pre-Christmas party. Since then she had put off going through her father's desk, finding it too painful a task. But it had to be done, so she opened another drawer and began to go through a pile of old letters and postcards she found there.

Most of these were from herself when she'd been to summer camp, and she threw them away, but presently she came to a card with a British stamp and a coloured picture of a pretty village with old houses of mellow golden stone set around a green square with an old-fashioned water pump. The sun shone on the flowers in the gardens and window-boxes, and there wasn't a car or a television aerial in sight. It looked such a tranquil scene, so different from the frenetically busy city where she lived in Canada.

Curiously Kelly turned the card over and found

5

that the village was called Ashdon Magna, in Gloucestershire. She smiled at the quaintness of the name, thinking how well it suited the picturesque village. Idly, almost, she began to read the postcard, but then straightened up in her chair, her body tense. The message was short but its import startling. It read: 'Dear Max,'—her father's name—' Just to let you know that our mutual great-aunt Lilian died last month. Thought you might like a pictorial reminder of your old hunting ground. Yours, Charles.'

So she did have some relations, after all! Kelly's hazel eyes lit with excitement. She knew that her parents had emigrated to Canada from England when she was still a baby, but she had never heard them speak of any relations and had thought she was now completely alone in the world. But obviously some members of her father's family were still living there. Or at least they were when the postcard was sent, which was . . . Kelly studied the rather blurred postmark and saw that the card was over ten years old. A long time. This man Charles might have moved away by now. Working it out in her head, Kelly decided that he must be her father's second cousin. Not a very close relation, but close enough perhaps to be informed of her father's death.

With an increasing feeling of interest and excitement that she hadn't felt since the day of the fatal crash, Kelly went on sorting through the piles of old letters, bills and diaries that her parents had left behind, trying to find further clues to this unknown relation. She had no luck however, until she came upon an old address book hidden among envelopes full of old photographs. Even then she almost missed it as she leafed through the pages looking for the name Charles. It was the word Ashdon that caught her eye and made her look more closely. And there it was in her father's spiky handwriting, shortened to: 'Chas Thorne, Ashdon Hall, A.M. Glos.' The A.M. presumably standing for Ashdon Magna.

With hardly a moment's hesitation, Kelly picked up a sheet of notepaper and began to write to her unknown relative, advising him of her parents' death and telling him something of herself. She also explained that she had only just discovered his existence and said that she would very much like to keep in touch and to learn more about her father's family. In her loneliness she could have written a lot more, but as it was there was almost a note of eager pleading in her letter. As soon as she'd finished it, Kelly braved the cold to go out and post the letter, her step brisker than it had been for weeks. What was this cousin of hers like? she wondered. Probably middle-aged now, as her father had been. But he might be married and have a family growing up in that beautiful village set among its green hills.

Often during the next weeks, as she waited eagerly for a reply, Kelly thought of that village. Somehow it had pulled at her heart-strings, filling her with nostalgia and a yearning for something she couldn't define. A need to get back to her roots, perhaps?

Kelly worked in a city bank and had been happy enough there until her parents' accident, but now she felt restless and grew increasingly unsettled as the days passed without her receiving a reply from Charles Thorne in England. There could be dozens of reasons for this, she knew: he could have moved house, be away on vacation, be busy, be dead even. But Kelly grew more impatient as the days passed and, after three weeks, on a sudden upsurge of rest-lessness, left her job.

What she needed, she decided, was a long vacation. Luckily she had plenty of money—no, not luckily—because she was only rich through her parents' deaths. They had both been heavily insured, and her father had also been an extremely successful businessman and entrepreneur, with a flair for knowing exactly what the market wanted at the right time. And now everything belonged to Kelly: the luxury apartment, the two cars in the basement garage, the log cabin up in the mountains for summer vacations, her mother's jewels and furs. But Kelly would willingly have traded every cent for her parents not to have gone to that party on the fateful night.

With a firmness that resisted the arguments of her lawyer and friends, Kelly sold the cars, put her parents' more personal possessions into store, leased the log cabin and the apartment, and packed for her vacation. She anticipated being away for at least six months and, although she told her friends that her plans were vague, Kelly knew exactly where she was going to go. To a village of old stone houses called Ashdon Magna.

The postcard hadn't lied. Kelly stood on the pavement where the noisy green bus had dropped her and took her first real look at the village. There were the stone houses, bright in the early spring sunlight, but with the gardens full of daffodils and narcissi now, their window-boxes empty, awaiting the summer. A light breeze blew, clearing the air of diesel fumes from the bus and filling her nostrils with a scent she had never smelt before but she knew

instinctively to be the smell of the land awakening
from the winter, ripe and ready to feed the seeds
sown into its richness to await the spring. She turned
and looked about her, saw the trees with fat buds,
ready to burst into glorious leaf, lambs with black
faces and bootees in the fields surrounding the hill
farms, heard a cuckoo sound in the woods behind
the high wall that bounded an estate on the edge of
the village. A feeling of coming home filled her, so
strong that for a few moments it hurt and made her
gasp. Even though she knew that she'd never been
here before, the feeling of *déjà vu* was incredibly
strong. It must be the postcard, Kelly decided. But
then a thought came to her: could this be where her
parents had lived when she was born? Might she
have sat in her baby-carriage in one of these
gardens, looking out at this street?

With a little smile at her own fancifulness, Kelly
picked up her suitcase and began to walk up the
street, to where she saw an inn sign swaying in the
wind. The same breeze caught at her dark curly hair
as she strode along, tall and graceful, her figure slim
but curvy in all the right places, especially under her
maple-leaf-emblazoned T-shirt, hidden now under
her padded anorak.

It was late afternoon, but there were quite a few
people about the village, gossiping outside the bow-
fronted village shop that had a red sign with 'Post
Office' written on it, or walking along. Several of
them glanced at Kelly curiously, but she was more
interested in looking at the pretty timber-framed
houses with their lattice windows and sagging roofs.

She walked slowly on down the street, often
pausing to admire, and presently came to the inn,
which she found was called the Horn of Plenty. The

only entrance seemed to be through the bar, so Kelly went inside, the conversation halting for a moment among the few people there as they saw her. The barman, thin but with strong arm muscles and a friendly smile, came up to her end of the bar. 'Good afternoon, miss.'

'Hi. Er—do you let rooms?'

He looked her over and nodded. 'Perhaps you'd like to speak to my wife.' He led her through a door into a hall with oak-beamed walls and ceiling. There was a smell of polish, and a big copper jug full of daffodils was set on an old chest against the wall. 'Claire,' the barman called, 'a customer for you.'

He nodded to Kelly and went back into the bar as his wife, brisk and smiling came to greet her. 'Hello, can I help you? I'm Mrs Trent.'

Kelly explained what she wanted and was taken upstairs to see a room set in one of the gables of the inn, a bright room with a flowered print wallpaper that matched the curtains and the hangings on the four-poster bed. It was thickly carpeted in pale green and furnished with antiques in soft, stripped pine. Kelly fell instantly in love with it and told Mrs Trent that she would take it without even bothering to ask the cost.

The older woman smiled at her eagerness. 'How long will you be staying?'

'I'm not quite sure at the moment. Definitely a couple of days, but maybe longer. Is the room available if I want it longer?'

'Oh, yes, you can have it as long as you like. We don't get many tourists this early in the year. You're American, aren't you?'

'No. I'm Ca . . .' Kelly hesitated, then laid claim to a nationality she had given little thought to before.

'I'm English. But I've lived in Canada most of my life.'

Later she had coffee in the oak-panelled dining-room of the inn, which was open to the general public but where only a dozen or so people were eating as it was a weekday.

'It's much busier at the weekend,' Mrs Trent told Kelly as she served her an apple turnover oozing with fresh cream. 'There's a small market here on Saturdays. And in the summer we get quite a few visitors on their way to the nearest stately home.'

'Is that Ashdon Hall?' Kelly asked, seizing such an apt opportunity.

'Oh, no, it's a mansion belonging to the National Trust a few miles from here, near Ashdon Parva. Ashdon Hall is the big house at the end of the village. But it isn't open to the public.'

'Is that the place with the high wall round it, near the bus stop?'

'Yes, that's right.' Claire Trent looked at her with interest. 'Have you been reading about it in the guide-books? It's supposed to be very old and interesting, although I've never been in it myself.'

'I've heard about it,' Kelly admitted. 'Don't the owners ever let people go around?'

'They open the gardens for charity a couple of days in the summer, but I've never heard of them opening the house.'

'Who are the owners? I heard that it was some-body called Charles Thorne,' Kelly suggested, fully expecting it to be denied.

'Yes, that's right,' Mrs Trent agreed easily, quite unaware of the effect it had on Kelly. 'The Thornes have lived at Ashdon Hall for hundreds of years. Fancy you knowing the name, though—I didn't think our village was that famous.'

'Oh, it's not. I mean . . .' Kelly flushed. 'I think my family came from somewhere around here. They must have told me.'

'So you're trying to trace your family, are you?' The landlady didn't seem at all surprised. 'We get a lot of foreigners doing that; mostly Americans, though. They usually go up to the church to look through the parish registers.'

Pleased at not being thought out of the ordinary, Kelly said, 'Maybe I'll do that.'

Mrs Trent went away to wait on someone else, leaving Kelly to finish her coffee and go outside. The breeze was stronger now and people were wrapped up against the cold, but to Kelly the weather was mild after the severity of a Canadian winter. Snug in her anorak, she stood for a moment under the creaking inn sign, but hesitated for only a few seconds before turning to walk in the direction of Ashdon Hall.

It took only about ten minutes to reach the imposing entrance, its wrought-iron gates flanked by stone pillars surmounted by heraldic beasts so time-worn that it was difficult to tell whether they were lions or leopards. There was a small house just behind it to the right, for the gatekeeper to live in, presumably, and a plain but neat sign saying, 'Ashdon Hall'.

The driveway was curved and very long, and Kelly could only catch a glimpse of tall chimneys beyond the still leafless trees that thickly lined it. Her first impulse was to go straight in and ask to see Charles Thorne, but she remembered that he hadn't replied to her letter. The reasons for this that she'd thought of back home obviously no longer applied if he was still living here. So why hadn't he answered? Even if he wasn't interested in her, he could at least have had the decency to acknowledge the news about her parents. On a sudden burst of righteous anger, Kelly pushed open the big iron gate and began to walk smartly up the driveway.

It must have been a quarter of a mile from the gate to the house, and Kelly was so interested in looking around her that a lot of her anger had evaporated by the time she reached it. The grounds were beautifully maintained, the trees interspersed with huge rhododendron bushes that would be a blaze of colour in a couple of months. Everything had a cared-for look about it, as if a great deal of time and effort had been put into the pleasing picture it made. The house, too, was beautiful. Kelly caught her breath as the driveway curved at last and the old stone building, glowing golden in the last of the fading sunlight, came into view, the sun reflecting on the latticed windows set between stone mullions. It was a large house but low, only two storeys and an attic, with little gabled windows which reminded Kelly of her room at the inn. Near the pillared doorway a creeper climbed almost up to the roof, its trunk so thick that it must have been nearly as old as the house.

For a moment the sheer richness and beauty of the place made her hesitate again. It was all so different from anything she had ever known, how could she possibly hope or expect to get along with the people who lived here, even if they were distant relations? She wondered if Charles Thorne had thought that too, and that was why he hadn't bothered to reply. But Kelly had a stubborn streak, and she certainly hadn't come all those thousands of miles to back down now, so she reached up and pulled the heavy metal bell-pull at the side of the door.

The door was so thick that she couldn't hear whether the bell had rung or not, but presently a woman wearing a blue nylon overall came in answer to her ring.

'Er—good morning. Are you Mrs Thorne?' Kelly asked, suddenly nervous.

'No, miss. There's no Mrs Thorne. I'm the housekeeper.'

'Oh. I'd like to see Mr Thorne, then, please.'

'I'm sorry, he isn't at home at the moment.'

'Oh. Well—er—when will he be back?'

'I've no idea, miss.' The housekeeper gave her a look of lively curiosity and said in her soft Gloucestershire accent, 'What would you be wanting him for, then?'

But Kelly had no intention of telling anyone other than Charles Thorne, so she said, 'I guess it can wait. I'll come back some other time. Perhaps you could just tell him that Kelly Baxter called?'

She turned to go but the woman said, 'Perhaps if you were to phone first, miss. Then you'd be sure of catching him at home.'

Kelly nodded. 'OK. Thanks.' She began to walk back down the driveway, but it was a moment or two before she heard the door shut behind her. The sun had gone down completely now, making the sky seem much darker and cooler. Kelly's step grew brisk as she thought about a log fire blazing in the dining-room back at the Horn of Plenty. And dinner. Already she felt hungry again. Mrs Trent had said they were serving a traditional dish called toad-in-the-hole tonight. Kelly wasn't sure she liked the sound of that. She'd thought it was only the

French who went in for frogs and snails and things.
But she was willing to try anything once. And after
dinner she would phone Ashdon Hall and see if Mr
Thorne would be home tomorrow morning and
would see her.

Her thoughts far away, Kelly was jerked violently
back to reality as a horse and rider suddenly burst
from between some bushes and on to the driveway
only a few yards ahead of her. She gave a cry of
fright and the horse shied, as startled as Kelly, but
was brought under immediate control by the man
who sat astride the big black stallion.

Instinctively Kelly raised her arms to protect her
face and backed away until brought up short by the
spreading branches of a tall conifer at the edge of the
drive.

The man quietened the horse and then turned
towards her. 'I'm sorry, I didn't realise . . .' He
stopped speaking abruptly and stared at her as she
stood in the shadows, his face and body stiffened into
stunned surprise. No, more than surprise, he looked
as if he'd received the shock of his life, his whole
being grew rigid with it and for a moment he seemed
turned to stone. 'Elaine!' The word was a strangled
cry, as if his voice, too, had been shocked into
numbness.

Then suddenly he was moving again, moving so
fast that he had leapt off the horse and was striding
towards her before Kelly realised what was
happening.

'Elaine.' He grabbed hold of her arms, his grip so
powerful that he hurt her. 'Where did you go? Why
did you go? My God, don't you know what I've
been through?'

Kelly tried to ward him off, petrified that she was

being attacked by some kind of maniac and hardly
hearing the torrent of questions he threw at her. But
her struggles only seemed to increase his anger and
the man shook her, sending her hair falling over her
face.

'Why did you just leave me like that? *Why*?
Without a word. Was I such a monster that you
couldn't even talk to me, tell me how you felt?'

He shook her again, fiercely, his fingers biting
into her even through the thickness of her jacket. But
suddenly fear changed into anger and Kelly struck
out at him, catching him in the face and taking
advantage of his instinctive sidestep to break free
and start to run. She didn't get very far. After only a
few yards the man caught her and spun her round.
Kelly recoiled from the fury in his face, but she had
found her voice and yelled, 'You keep the hell away
from me!' She backed away from him, her arm out-
stretched as if her puny strength could hold him off.

He gave a snarl of rage and came after her, but as
she stepped into the pool of light from one of the
lamps he suddenly checked, his eyes widening incredulously. Kelly took another few steps, her pace
quickening as she wondered whether to try and hide
among the trees or cut and run back to the house,
but then the man moved swiftly forward and caught
her again. Kelly opened her mouth to scream, but he
quickly covered it with his hand. She stared up into
his eyes, dark eyes that glinted fiercely down at her,
and felt her senses begin to swim. Oh, God, she
thought. Oh, God, he's going to kill me. His grip
tightened and he dragged her nearer the lamp.

'But you're not . . . Just who are you?' the man
demanded on a note of thunderstuck amazmnt.

'What?' Kelly stared at him, still too terrified to

think straight.

'I said, who are you? You're not El . . . You're not who I thought you were.'

Slowly it penetrated that he'd mistaken her for someone else. Carefully, her eyes on his face, Kelly stepped away from the man, and this time he let go of her. She gave a shuddering sigh of relief and kept on backing away.

'Wait. Look, I didn't mean to . . .'

But Kelly didn't wait to hear any more, all she could think of was to get away from this madman, as far and as quickly as possible. He stretched out a restraining hand towards her and she screamed and fled, faster than she'd ever run in her life.

'Stop! Don't go.'

The man's shout gave extra strength to her legs and Kelly pelted along the driveway, only realising which way she'd been running when she arrived at the gate near the village. Even then she didn't stop, but hared across the road and towards the lights of the houses, afraid even to look behind to see if he was chasing her.

Only when she reached the inn did she stop, her legs aching painfully, her breath raw and rasping in her throat. She gave an agonised look behind her but the man wasn't there, the village street was empty and deserted and the pounding footsteps that she'd thought were following her turned out to be only the thudding of her own heart. Kelly leaned against the wall, fighting for breath, her body still shaking with terror. I'm going home, she thought incoherently. I'm catching the first plane out of here and I'm going home. My God, and I thought this was a peaceful place!

Claire Trent had shown her the residents entrance

at the side of the inn and she stumbled towards it.
There was no one around and she went slowly up to
her room and collapsed on the bed. She lay there
until her heart was back to normal, the heat of anger
and indignation helping a lot. That maniac! He
ought to be locked away some place. But then she
remembered that the man had called her Elaine and
said he'd mistaken her for someone else. Kelly took
off her anorak and rubbed her bruised arms,
thankful that she hadn't been the real Elaine,
because that man, whoever he was, had been
murderously angry. Fleetingly she wondered what
this girl, Elaine, must have done to provoke such
terrible rage, but her hands were still shaking and
Kelly decided she needed a stiff brandy. There was
no drinks cupboard in the room and the inn didn't
run to a phone for room service, so she changed
quickly and went down to the little bar reserved for
residents. It was empty and Mr Trent quickly served
her drink and went away to attend to customers in
the other bar. Kelly sank into a chair by the fire, and
it was only when the first couple of swallows of the
brandy had gone gratefully down that it occurred to
her that her assailant might quite easily have been
the relation she was looking for, Charles Thorne!

The brandy worked wonders. Kelly stopped
shaking and began to go over the incident at Ashdon
Hall without the fear that had numbed her brain
before. And now, of course, it seemed far less
terrifying. The man, whoever he was, had mistaken
her for someone else in the darkness, someone he
hadn't expected to see and with whom he was
obviously furiously angry. But now Kelly
remembered that once he'd realised he'd made a
mistake the man had let her go. So maybe he wasn't

a maniac, after all. But God, she'd been so scared. Never before, she was sure, had she seen such murderous rage in anyone's face.

Kelly trembled in remembrance and went up to the bar to get another drink. She didn't usually have two drinks before dinner, and definitely not brandy, but brandy was supposed to be good for shock and she decided she definitely warranted it tonight.

Mr Trent was busy serving a crowd of people who'd arrived to play a darts match with the local team, and she had to wait until he noticed her. From here Kelly could see a part of the now noisy public bar, and on the right through to the corridor with the stairs leading up to the guest rooms and the residents entrance. As she waited the residents' door opened and she glanced across. A man walked in, tall, with thick, dark hair. He was about thirty and handsome in a hard, masculine kind of way, with level brows, straight nose and strong jawline. And dark grey eyes that Kelly had more than enough cause to remember. As she stared at him the man who had attacked her earlier looked round and saw her. Immediately he strode to the bar, opened the door and came in.

Kelly grabbed a heavy glass ashtray from the bar and held it threateningly. 'You keep away from me!' she exclaimed fearfully.

But the man held up his hand placatingly. 'Please don't be alarmed,' he said quickly. 'I've come to apologise. I'm not going to hurt you.'

Kelly eyed him distrustfully, but in the light he looked completely different from the furious man who had been so rough with her. The anger was gone from his eyes now, to be replaced by a frown of troubled concern. He was still wearing riding clothes; polished boots, tight-fitting breeches, and a riding-jacket that emphasised his broad frame, but he wore them with an elegantly casual air. In fact, he looked so civilised that it was hard to imagine that he could have so completely lost control of himself back there at Ashdon Hall. Slowly, Kelly lowered the ashtray. The man's frown eased a little and he said, 'I'm extremely sorry about what happened. I'm afraid I mistook you for someone else. It was dark, you see, and I was—was taken by surprise. I hadn't expected . . .' He broke off and gave a small jerk of his head, as if trying to shake off a memory, and his voice was more in control as he went on. 'The fact is that you strongly resemble someone I used to know. At first I thought you were her, but when I saw you in the light of course I realised my mistake.' His eyes went to her face. But evidently the memory of the other girl was painful and he drew himself up. 'So I came at once to tell you how sorry I am,' he said stiffly. 'I hope that I didn't hurt you in any way.'

Kelly thought of the bruises there would be on her arms tomorrow. 'You scared the hell out of me,' she said sharply.

'Yes, I imagine I must have done. If there's anything I can do to make up for . . .'

'You can buy me another brandy,' Kelly interrupted as the landlord came round to the bar. And she went back to sit by the fire.

The man exchanged a few words with Mr Trent and then came over to her and set the glass of brandy on the table in front of her. He had also bought himself a drink that looked like a pretty stiff whisky. Maybe he felt in need of something to get over the shock, too. He looked at her for a moment, the frown back between his eyes, and Kelly guessed that he was hating this. Not that he'd made a mistake and had to apologise, but the fact that he had completely lost control of his emotions, and she, a stranger, had seen and now had to be given an explanation.

'My name's Thorne,' he said shortly. 'I live at Ashdon Hall.'

So he *was* her relation. But he was a much younger man than Kelly had expected. Her father had been fifty and she'd thought that his cousin would be the same age, but she was evidently wrong. 'How did you find me?' she asked, wondering if he knew who she was.

'You're a stranger to the village, and you spoke with an American accent. It wasn't difficult to guess that any American visitor would be staying here at the inn.'

So he hadn't been back to the house and learned that she had left her name. He must have caught and seen to his horse and then come right after her. 'I see.'

She hesitated, wondering what to do, wondering if she wanted to claim the relationship at all now. But the decision was taken out of her hands when her cousin said, 'Did you have business at the Hall? Can I help you in any way?'

His tone was polite, courteous, but just a little withdrawn, and Kelly guessed that he wanted to get this over with and go. He was being civil because he felt he owed it to her, but he didn't really want to know her. And he hadn't answered her letter either. The thought angered Kelly and she gave him a cold look. 'Yes, I had business at the Hall. With you, as a matter of fact.'

'With me?' His left eyebrow arched. 'May I sit

down?'

Kelly nodded, her eyes widening at the complexity of a man who could grab hold of you and shake the life out of you, but who wouldn't sit down until he was invited.

'And why did you want to see me, Miss . . .?' He left the question hanging after glancing at her ringless left hand.

'Baxter.' Kelly said clearly. 'Kelly Baxter. From Canada. I wrote you a few weeks ago.'

He had frowned at the sound of her name, evidently not recognising it, but when she mentioned the letter his brow cleared. 'Ah yes, I remember.' His eyes went over her again, as if assessing her in a different light.

Kelly waited for him to go on but he didn't; the silence became awkward, so she said stubbornly, 'I think that we must be kind of cousins.'

He gave a slow nod, as if his mind was elsewhere. 'Yes, that might account for the likeness. It's possible.' But suddenly he became brisk and said, 'No, Miss Baxter, you didn't write to me.'

'But I did,' Kelly interrupted before he could go on. 'It was about a month ago. Unless you didn't get the letter. I certainly didn't get any reply.'

'No, you misunderstand me,' he told her with an impatient gesture. 'The letter was received but it wasn't sent to me. It was sent to Charles Thorne.'

'But you said you were Charles Thorne!'

'No, I'm sorry. I'm Byron Thorne. Charles Thorne is a very distant relation of mine. I'm from a different branch of the family.'

'But you—you said you live at the Hall,' Kelly protested in confusion.

'Yes, I do.' He hesitated, then said, 'I've taken

over the management of the Hall estates. You see
Charles Thorne was very badly injured in an
accident a couple of years ago and is now a cripple.'

'And did that stop him answering my letter?'
Kelly demanded.

'No.' Byron Thorne hesitated again, obviously
reluctant to talk about such personal matters. 'But
the letter came to me and I decided not to show it to
him.'

Kelly gave him an indignant look. 'And just what
right have you to do that?'

'Charles was in hospital for an operation and I
was dealing with his correspondence. And to be
honest I . . .'

'Yes, do be honest, Mr Thorne,' Kelly
interrupted acidly.

His face hardened and he said curtly, 'I decided
that hearing about the death of relatives, however
distant, was more than he could handle at the time.'

'And now? Is he still in hospital?'

'No.' Byron shook his head reluctantly. 'But he
has enough—problems at the moment, without
adding to them.'

Kelly's chin came up. 'And just what makes you
think that I might be a problem?'

His mouth twisted wryly. 'You're obviously very
impetuous. Coming here to England like this without even knowing if Charles wanted to see you, or
even if he was still living here. It's hardly a
responsible thing to do.'

'What I do is my affair,' Kelly answered shortly, a
flush of indignant colour in her pale cheeks. 'And as
far as I can see you have absolutely no right to keep
my letter from *my cousin Charles*,' she said,
emphasising the relationship,

Byron's eyes darkened impatiently. 'Look, I don't know why you're here, but . . .'

'To find out about my father's family,' Kelly broke in. 'And as I've come a very long way, I don't intend to leave until I've talked to Charles Thorne,' she told him shortly, her voice rising.

A flash of anger shone in Byron's eyes, but he mastered it and said with exaggerated patience, 'Look, Miss Baxter, if it's your family history you want to find out about, then I'll help you all I can. Get someone to find out where in England you should go to look up the parish registers and that sort of thing, but I would much rather you didn't see Charles.'

'Why not?' Kelly demanded bluntly.

'There are reasons—private reasons,' he added quickly before she could ask. 'I must ask you to take my word for it that it would not be—wise for you to see him.'

'Your word?' Kelly said disparagingly, angry that she was being fobbed off in this way.

Byron's chin came up and for a moment she had a glimpse of the anger he had shown earlier, but this anger was cold and controlled, not hot with the fury and pain with which he'd attacked her. Pain? Yes, she realised now that there had been the rawness of pain behind his rage. Again she wondered who Elaine was and what she had done to him. Almost she opened her mouth to ask, but then shut it again, aware that he would shut her out from his personal life so coldly that her blood would freeze in her veins. 'Yes, my word, he grated challengingly. 'Well, will you accept my offer of help?'

'I might.'

He frowned. 'And will you agree not to trouble

Charles Thorne?'

'I might,' Kelly repeated, annoyed that he should describe her as a troublemaker.

He looked at the defiant set of her mouth and stood up so that she had to tilt her head back to look at him. 'I'm sorry that you have had such an unfortunate introduction to Ashdon Magna,' he said formally. 'How long do you intend to stay?'

'Just as long as it takes,' Kelly said stubbornly.

His mouth twisted, but Byron said shortly, 'My offer is still open.'

'How very kind of you,' she answered with mock sweetness.

He gave her an angry, frowning look, as if he found her attitude baffling. A lock of his thick, dark hair had fallen forward, and as he pushed it back Kelly noticed a ring, a heavy gold signet, on his left hand. Was he married, then? Was Elaine his wife? The thought intrigued her, and so did Byron Thorne, she realised, as he gave her a curt nod goodnight and walked away. He looked the kind of man who could handle any situation—or any woman, but Elaine, whoever she was, had evidently got deep under his skin. Outwardly he seemed capable and confident, a man who had already got where he was going; qualities that gave him a magnetism that would be hard to resist. But Kelly had been given a brief glimpse of the deep emotional feelings that lay beneath his self-assurance. They both knew it, and it was quite plain that Byron bitterly resented it. And that, she thought, was the real reason why he was trying to fob her off. But she hadn't travelled all those hundreds of miles to just turn and go meekly home. She had come to find her only relation and she was darned if Byron Thorne, or anyone else, was going to stop her!

Going quickly out to the telephone booth, Kelly looked up the number of Ashdon Hall and rang it. It was answered almost at once by a woman whose voice sounded like that of the housekeeper. 'Oh, hello. This is Kelly Baxter. Do you remember I called at the house earlier? Yes, I just wanted to make it clear that it was Mr *Charles* Thorne I wanted to see. Yes, that's right. And will you tell him please that I'm Maxwell Baxter's daughter, and that I've come over from Canada to see him. You're sure you've got that right? OK, thanks. And you will be sure to tell him straight away, won't you? Now? Oh, that's great. Thanks. Goodbye.' And Kelly put the phone down triumphantly.

CHAPTER TWO

AT DINNER, Kelly found that the toad-in-the-hole was actually sausages cooked in a light, crispy batter. Different, definitely, and quite tasty, but she wasn't sure she liked her sausages cooked in a waffle. There weren't many other people in the dining-room, so Claire Trent had time to talk to her a little, asking her how she'd enjoyed her walk round the village.

'It looks very pretty,' Kelly answered.

'And have you managed to trace any of your ancestors yet?'

'No, not yet.' Not an ancestor, no, but one distant relation who was very much alive, Kelly thought, thinking of Byron and realising that if he was related to Charles Thorne he was also related to her. But he'd said a different branch of the family; she wondered when the branch had grown out from the family tree and just how remote a relative he was.

The phone rang out in the hall and Mrs Trent went to answer it. A moment later she came back and said to Kelly in a voice loaded with curiosity. 'There's a phone call for you. It's Ashdon Hall.'

'Oh, thanks.' Kelly went out into the hall to take the call, but picked up the receiver gingerly, realising that Byron had had time to get back home by now and find out that she'd telephoned. 'Hello,' she said warily, 'Kelly Baxter here.'

But it was a woman's voice that said, 'Hello

27

again, Miss Baxter. This is Mrs Banks, Mr Thorne's housekeeper. I gave Mr Thorne your message and he would like to see you. He asks if you can come up to the house tonight for an hour or so? Would eight-thirty be too early for you?'

'Why, no, that would be fine,' Kelly said eagerly.

'Oh, good. He won't keep you very late; he keeps early hours. And he'll have someone walk you back to the Horn.'

'Oh, that's OK, he doesn't have to do that,' Kelly replied, after she'd worked out that the Horn must be the local name for the inn.

But Mrs Banks said, 'We'll expect you at eight-thirty, then.'

Kelly replaced the receiver with a small smile. So much for Byron and his 'keep off' orders. He might be used to English women who obeyed his every command, but she definitely wasn't one of them. Not that she had any intention of imposing on her cousin Charles; she just wanted to meet him and perhaps learn a little about her father's family, but if she thought that he seemed too ill or tired she would leave at once.

At eight-fifteen, Kelly went up to her room to get her coat, carefully checking her appearance in the mirror and brushing her dark curls from her face. She looked at herself in the mirror for a moment, wondering if she was very much like the mysterious Elaine, and whether she would find out who she was tonight. Because she had to admit that she was more than a little intrigued by this girl who could arouse such passion in the very austere Byron Thorne.

It was completely dark now, but there was light enough from the ornate streetlamps, hung with baskets of flowers, for her to see her way. There were

lanterns, too, attached to the stone pillars on either
side of the gateway to the hall, and the antique
copper lamp-posts that lined the drive. Kelly walked
briskly, wondering exactly where it had been that
Byron had ridden out earlier. She shivered and
turned up her collar, although she told herself firmly
that there was nothing to be afraid of. But she was
glad to reach the front door and ring the bell,
preferring to face the unknown Charles Thorne than
think of the encounter with Byron.

The housekeeper, Mrs Banks, Kelly remembered,
opened the door to her with a friendly smile. 'Do
come in, miss. Let me take your coat. It's been a
windy day, hasn't it? But you'll soon be warm
again. Mr Charles always has a nice fire burning in
the evenings.' She hung Kelly's coat in a cupboard,
still chattering. 'This way, miss.' She led Kelly
down a bright hallway, the panelling painted white,
into a room at the back of the house.

It was a large room, lined with shelves full of
books and records. Thick velvet curtains were drawn
to shut out the April chill and the fire that Mrs
Banks had promised flamed in a big old fireplace,
but the room was dominated by a high-backed wing
chair set on one side of the fire—or rather by the
man who sat in it. He was grey-haired and his face
was lined, but he still had the frame of a man who
had once been broad and strong. Whether he was
very tall was difficult to tell, but his arms and
shoulders were still powerful, although he had a
tartan rug covering his legs. And he was handsome,
too, except where the lines of suffering had deepened
his eyes and pulled down his mouth. For a moment
Kelly thought she saw something of Byron in his
profile, but the impression was swiftly gone as he

turned to greet her.

There was an amiable smile of welcome on his face, but this changed to a fixed stare as she walked towards him.

'Hi,' Kelly said uncertainly.

Charles Thorne blinked, recovered, and held out his hand. 'How do you do, Miss Baxter? How very kind of you to come and see me. Won't you sit down?'

He indicated a chair opposite his and Kelly looked at him more closely as she took it. He looked as if he had been ill; his skin was very pale and the lines of pain were etched deep, but his eyes were bright and intelligent, full of life, although there was a hard set to his face, as if he could be very severe and demanding. Kelly had the feeling that he set himself high standards and expected others to do the same. Not an easy man to live with, perhaps, especially now that he was crippled. But he was pleasant enough as he smiled and said, 'So you're Maxwell's daughter. You have the family likeness. And how are your parents? It must be more than twenty years since they emigrated.'

'You—you don't know?' Kelly looked at him rather helplessly, realising that as Byron had kept her letter from him she would have to explain herself, and not wanting to. 'My parents—they're dead. They were killed in a car accident just before Christmas.' She said it quickly to get it over, forcing the grief down, and going hastily on. 'I wrote you, but I guess—I guess you didn't get my letter. And I felt like a holiday so I thought I'd come on over. I've never been to England before. I found your address in Pop's papers and I thought I'd start here. I hope you don't mind?'

She had said too much and too quickly, but

Charles Thorne seemed to understand, and he didn't give her soft-voiced sympathy, thank goodness—Kelly had had too much of that from well-meaning friends lately. He simply said with genuine feeling, 'I am very sorry to hear that, but very glad you decided to come here. I expect you want to find out all about your family, don't you? I seem to remember you're an only child?' And, when Kelly nodded, 'Yes, I thought so. Well, I'm afraid I can't tell you much about your mother's side because she didn't come from round here. I think she came from London originally, but your father met her at university. But your father I can tell you about. I knew him quite well when he was young.'

A reminiscent smile came into his eyes for a moment, but then he recollected himself and said, 'I'm so sorry, would you like a drink? Perhaps you'd like to pour yourself something from the tray over there. I'm stuck in this chair and can't do the honours myself. And perhaps you'd also be good enough to pour me a small dry sherry. That's the most I'm allowed, I'm afraid.'

As Kelly went to get the drinks she saw a wheelchair nearby and realised that this room must be his sanctum, the place where he spent his life with his books and music. As she gave him the drink she said, 'I'm sorry to see that you've had an accident, too.' She hesitated for a moment, but saw that because he had been matter of fact about her parents' accident she could be too. So she said, 'Was it a car smash?'

'Mm? Oh, no. I walked in front of a truck. Wasn't looking where I was going.'

He didn't elaborate but began talking about Kelly's father who, it seemed, had quite often

stayed here when he was a boy. 'Your father and I
were about the same age,' he said. 'And he was sent
to school not far from here. He was an only child, of
course, and he was sent to boarding-school because
his parents were abroad for several years, so he used
to come and stay with us during the holidays. He
was quite a young devil, I remember, always getting
into mischief.' He told Kelly about some of her
father's escapades, which made her laugh delightedly.

Charles Thorne broke off when she laughed,
looking at her with a wistfulness so deep that it
seemed to give him pain. But then he recollected
himself. 'Where was I? It's just that for a moment
you reminded me of—someone I used to know.'

He went on with his story, but Kelly's thoughts
wandered. Evidently he, too, must know this Elaine
that she resembled so closely. Kelly's eyes slid
around the room, noting the number of framed
photographs on walls and shelves. Did any of them
picture someone like her? But it was impossible to
see from a distance, and she didn't want to appear
rude by peering at them. So she turned her attention
back to Mr Thorne's anecdotes and soon forgot
about Elaine.

Listening to stories about her father led to her
telling some, and then Kelly found herself talking
about her life in Canada, of herself, and how she had
found the postcard and decided to come to England.
'Perhaps I shouldn't have come when I didn't hear
from you, but I—I needed to get away for a while.'

Charles Thorne nodded. 'Yes, I can understand
that. You were right to come here. Who else should
you turn to but your own family?'

Kelly gave him a grateful look, but said ruefully,

'I guess it would be kind of pushy to say I'm family when we've never met before.'

'Nonsense. I'm very glad you're here. In fact, you must come and stay. Do you ride? We have some good horses in the stables.'

'Oh, but I couldn't do that,' Kelly protested. 'I only came to meet you. I don't intend for you to ask me to stay.'

'Well, I am,' her cousin said firmly. 'And I very much hope that you will accept. It will be pleasant to have some feminine company aga——' He broke off, his face suddenly sagging and looking old, but before Kelly could begin to be alarmed he recovered himself and said, 'for a change.'

She was briefly puzzled, but too overwhelmed by his invitation to take much notice. She wondered what Byron's reaction would be when he knew. Certainly not a glad one. He definitely wouldn't want her to stay. And, as Kelly tended to be obstinate by nature, this fact alone would probably have decided her to accept, but also she wanted to for her own sake. She wanted to see more of this beautiful house, of the village, and of this lovely area of England. And she wanted to be in a place and among people who didn't constantly remind her of the life she had lost when her parents were killed, or to be overloaded with kindness and sympathy. And the latter at least she was sure she wouldn't get here; Charles Thorne had learned to be as matter of fact about death as he had about his own terrible disability, and Byron Thorne, Kelly was sure, didn't have an ounce of sympathy in his make-up. But could she live in the same house as Byron? Kelly wasn't sure but, if she found she couldn't, she could always leave. And besides, by staying here, she

would probably find it much easier to solve the
mystery of the girl Elaine. So she smiled at her host
and said, 'Well, if you're really sure it wouldn't be
too much trouble?'

'Of course not. You'll stay? Good. Come tomorrow. I'll have Mrs Banks prepare a room for you.'

He talked for a little about all the interesting
places she could visit in the area, but began to look
tired; Kelly felt she ought to go, that to talk any
longer would be too much for him. She was just
about to say so and get to her feet when the door
opened and Byron Thorne strode into the room. He
saw her and, after a first check of surprise, his face
became a contained mask of anger.

'Ah, Byron,' Charles said to him, 'I'd like you to
meet a young relative of mine. And of yours too, I
suppose, if we go back into history. My cousin
Maxwell's daughter, Kelly Baxter. And this, Kelly,
is Byron Thorne, who has been kind enough to come
and take care of things for me since I've
been—incapacitated.'

Byron closed the door and took a couple of steps
into the room, but didn't come any nearer. 'Miss
Baxter,' he said shortly.

'Mr Thorne,' she answered equally coldly.

'Kelly is from Canada,' Charles Thorne told
Byron, apparently unaware of the tension. 'She's
staying at the Horn of Plenty at the moment, but has
very kindly consented to come and stay here with
us.'

Byron gave her a shrivelling look. 'Has she,
indeed? As you say, how *very* kind of her.'

Kelly got to her feet and gave him back a cool
glance in return. 'Do you live here, too, Mr
Thorne?'

'Oh, call him Byron,' Charles interrupted. 'We're not that formal, not even in England, you know.'

'All right, Byron.' She smiled at Charles Thorne. 'And I shall call you Cousin Charles.'

'How very cosy,' Byron said with a smooth mockery that made her angry.

To pay him back and put him in a position of guilt, she said mendaciously, 'Such a pity that you didn't get my letter, Cousin Charles. It must have got lost in the post.'

She threw Byron a challenging look as she said it, sure that he would duck the blame, but she had underestimated him. Walking over to the older man, he said calmly. 'It didn't get lost. It arrived when you were in hospital and I decided to shelve it until I thought you were well enough to deal with it. Miss Baxter, however, obviously couldn't wait to meet you.'

He said it with a cynical look in his dark eyes, a look hidden from his cousin.

'Did you, indeed?' Charles Thorne said curtly. 'But as this was nothing to do with the estate, you shouldn't have taken the decision on yourself.' There was authority in his voice, and Kelly saw that he was still the master of his own household, if not of his own frail body.

'Very well.' Byron was in no way put out, but the glance he gave Kelly suddenly made her feel chilled through to her bones.

She said quickly. 'I guess I'd better be going. It's been a long day.'

'Of course. I mustn't keep you. But I'll see you tomorrow morning, then,' her cousin said, and added, 'Byron will see you safely back to the Horn.'

'Oh, no, that really isn't necessary,' Kelly said in consternation. 'I don't need . . .'

But Charles Thorne had closed his eyes wearily and Byron was holding the door open for her. After a moment of unhappy indecision, Kelly said goodnight and walked through into the hall. Byron closed the door and followed her. 'Did you have a coat?'

'Yes. Your housekeeper put it in a cupboard.'

But Byron had already taken it out and was holding it for her. Kelly was tempted to tell him that she could manage on her own, but realised that this was a courtesy that came completely naturally to him, whoever the woman happened to be. She let him help her, but said stiffly as he went to put on his own coat. 'Thanks, but I don't need anyone to go with me. I'll be OK by myself.'

'I expect you will, but Charles has asked me to see you home.'

'I'm hardly likely to be attacked *twice* in one night,' she pointed out with heavy irony.

Byron's eyebrows drew into a frown. 'Isn't describing it as being attacked rather an over-exaggeration?'

'Not if you look as the bruises on my arms, it's not,' Kelly retorted. 'I'm just glad I wasn't this Elaine—whoever she is.'

She left the end of the sentence poised as a question but Byron didn't offer any explanation. His face just tightened and he said, 'Again, I can only apologise.' He walked to the front door and opened it. 'If you're ready?'

She walked towards him but said, 'I'd prefer to go alone, if you don't mind.'

'But I do mind.' His dark eyes swept over her

sardonically. 'So Charles has invited you to stay. And you—naturally—have accepted.'

'And why shouldn't I accept?' Kelly said belligerently.

'I've already told you that there were reasons for you to keep away from him.' Byron closed the door firmly behind them and began to walk briskly down the driveway. He was tall and long-legged, and he made no attempt to shorten his stride for her as she fell in beside him, but Kelly was young and fit and had little difficulty in keeping up.

'But you wouldn't tell me what the reasons are,' she pointed out. 'So I decided to find out for myself. But Cousin Charles seemed very pleased to meet me. We talked for quite some time and . . .'

'What about?' Byron interrupted.

'Why, about my father mostly. It seemed he often used to stay here when he was young. Why do you . . .?'

'And that was all?' Byron gave her no time to finish. 'He didn't talk about—anyone else?'

'Not especially,' His voice had sharpened, and Kelly looked at him keenly, but it was too dark to see his face clearly. Not, she thought, that she would have learned anything anyway; Byron was too good at hiding his feelings for that. 'Why? Who do you think he might have talked about?' she probed.

He shrugged non-committally. 'I just wondered.'

Trying to keep her tone offhand, Kelly said, 'Perhaps, if I'm going to stay here, it might be a good idea if you told me *why* you thought I shouldn't meet Cousin Charles?'

Byron turned his head to look at her and his mouth twisted wryly. 'Are you always this inquisitive?'

Kelly looked offended. 'I just wanted to be sure not to say anything wrong—anything that might upset him. But that might be difficult when I don't know what it is I'm not supposed to talk about,' she pointed out.

They paused under a lamp-post and she saw Byron give her a moody kind of look. For a moment she thought that he was going to tell her, but then he gave a negative shake of his head and said, 'It doesn't matter. It's probably too late now, anyway.'

'What is?' Kelly demanded exasperatedly. 'Why all the big mystery?'

They had reached the main gate and he paused. 'There's no mystery,' he said on a harsh note that belied his words. 'But now that you've wormed your way in here, I'd just be grateful if you'll remember that Charles is still very much a sick man. He gets depressed sometimes. And I don't want him upset unnecessarily. Do you understand?'

'No,' Kelly answered baldly. 'I don't. And I don't understand why you're so against me coming to visit here, either. Are you always this unfriendly?'

'I am merely trying to protect Charles.'

'Protect him? Well, it doesn't seem to me that he's so ill he can't make up his own mind about who he wants or doesn't want to meet. It's only his body that's disabled, isn't it, not his mind and . . .'

But Byron had turned impatiently away and began to walk quickly on, lengthening his stride so that she had to run to keep up with him. 'You know nothing of the matter,' he said shortly. 'But I can hardly expect you to show any sensitivity when you've already expressly gone against my request for you to stay away from Charles.'

'Request?' Kelly exclaimed derisively, his tone

rousing her to immediate antagonism. 'You mean *command*. But I don't take orders, and if you won't give explanations then you have no right to give orders.'

They had come to the door of the inn, and Byron turned to face her, as angry as she. 'I can't stop Charles from inviting you to stay at the Hall, and I can't stop you from accepting but I warn you, Miss Baxter, if I . . .'

'Kelly,' she interrupted him with flippant mockery, tired of his overbearing manner. 'Don't you remember? Cousin Charles said we were related, too. And after all, if we're going to be living in the same house it seems silly to be so formal—or so unfriendly,' she added deliberately.

He eyed her sardonically, a grim smile twisting his lips. 'I'm beginning to think you're very clever—and possibly very dangerous.'

Kelly looked at him and slowly shook her head. 'No,' she said in a low voice. 'I'm neither of those things.' She was about to add that she was just very lonely, but you couldn't make that kind of a confession to someone who showed as much antipathy as Byron. His lip would only curl in that sardonic way he had and he would refuse to believe her.

He laughed scornfully. 'Well, I'm sure I'm going to find out one way or another. But either way I'm going to wish you'd stayed in Canada where you belong—and maybe,' he added forcefully, 'you'll come to wish it too.' He nodded curtly. 'Goodnight to you.' And he swung on his heel and left her to go into the inn alone.

It was mostly feelings of puzzlement that kept Kelly awake that night. She lay in the cosy bed, listening to the wind outside and wondering why

Byron was so sure that she would upset Cousin Charles. The only reason she could think of was because she resembled the girl Byron had mistaken her for, Elaine. Presumably he'd thought that the resemblance would upset Charles, too. So Elaine must have been important in both their lives. But it had been Byron whose emotions had swamped him, who had fired agonised questions at her and wanted the answers so badly that he had shaken her in his fury. Charles Thorne had seen the resemblance too, but he had seen her first in a good light instead of the darkness outside, so perhaps it wasn't such a shock for him. Or perhaps the thought of Elaine didn't stir up such an emotional reaction as it did in Byron. Unless Charles was even better at hiding his feelings. He certainly seemed to be a very reserved kind of man. But Kelly had quite liked him and she had enjoyed hearing about her father's boyish escapades.

She wondered if she was going to enjoy her stay at Ashdon Hall. The inanimate things, yes: the house and its old furniture, the garden and the village. But the two men who lived there? That sharp old man who for some inexplicable reason hadn't looked where he was going and had been crippled because of it. And Byron, who had come to take over the management of the estate and who said he wanted to protect him, even from letters that he might find distressing. But Charles hadn't been upset; he had been almost stoical about his cousin's death. And surely Byron must have known that he would be.

Byron was, Kelly decided, a very puzzling person. He seemed used to having his own way and to being obeyed. Hardly surprising, really, if he was used to running an estate. Although Kelly had no clear idea

how big the estate was, she had gained the
impression that it was quite a responsibility. What
had he done for a living before he came to Ashdon
Hall? she wondered. And who was Elaine? Why did
she mean so much to him? Sleep began to claim her,
but Kelly dimly remembered Mrs Banks saying that
there was no Mrs Thorne. But Byron could have
been married before he came here. He was certainly
attractive enough to be married, she mused
dreamily. His image filled her mind. His height and
the breadth of his shoulders. His strong body and
dark good looks. And his hard, clean-cut face and
cold, dark eyes. She wondered if he smiled much
and what he would look like if he did. Her eyes
opened and Kelly gazed up at the patterns of
moonlight on the ceiling. She had been so busy
arguing with Byron that she hadn't thought about
him as a man, but it seemed that he had had quite an
effect on her, because she could still picture him in
her mind, sharp in every detail. Not that it
mattered, of course, because he'd made it plain that
he didn't want her around. And, anyway, he was
obviously deeply involved with Elaine. Whoever she
was. Tomorrow, Kelly thought; I'll ask Mrs Banks
tomorrow. And she drifted into sleep.

There were kippers for breakfast next morning.
Kelly was almost put off when she enquired what
they were and Claire Trent said smoked herrings,
but on the theory that when in England you did what
the English did, she tried them and was glad she did.
They were delicious, hot and tasty and oozing with
melted butter, although Kelly found picking out all
the bones a drawback.

'How did you like them?' Mrs Trent asked when
she came to collect Kelly's plate.

'They were fine. I enjoyed them. I'll be leaving this morning, by the way,' she added.

'No luck tracing your ancestors?'

'Some. As a matter of fact, it turns out that Mr Thorne at the Hall is a relative of mine.'

'Really? That's why you were with Byron, then.'

It occured to Kelly that as the landlady of the inn Mrs Trent would know all the local gossip. 'You know Byron?'

'Oh, yes, we know most of the people who live around here. Although we're strangers really. We've only been here for seven years.'

Kelly's eyes widened. 'But how can you still be strangers after seven years?'

Mrs Trent laughed. 'Oh, that's nothing. Unless you've lived here for at least three generations, you're thought of as newcomers by the villagers.'

'But I expect you hear about everything that goes on?' Kelly said as casually as she could.

'Most things,' her companion admitted. 'There aren't many scandals that don't get talked about after a few drinks in the bar.'

'Are there many scandals in a peaceful village like this?'

'Oh, you'd be surprised. Villages are hotbeds of gossip.'

'And I suppose the local lord of the manor is a prime target?' Kelly hinted hopefully.

'Sometimes.' The other woman gave her a shrewd look. 'Not that there's much going on at the moment. I expect everyone will be interested in you when they find out you're staying at the Thornes'.'

'I didn't say I was staying with them,' Kelly remarked.

'You didn't have to. Mrs Banks rang earlier to say

that they'd send a car to collect you at ten-thirty. And she also said that Mr Thorne would take care of your bill.'

Kelly's eyes had widened, but now she said firmly, 'I can't let Mr Thorne do that. I'll pay for it myself.'

'Oh, I shouldn't worry.' Claire Trent stood up. 'We're only the tenants here, you know. The inn and most of the village is part of the Ashdon Hall estate.'

'It's that big?' Kelly asked, feeling stunned.

'Huge. There are several farms and stretches of open land and woods, as well as a couple more villages, that I know of. So you see, I can't afford to offend my landlord by letting you pay your own bill, now can I?' And she grinned as she went away to attend to another guest.

A car driven by a chauffeur who introduced himself as Jim Banks, the housekeeper's husband, arrived on the dot of ten-thirty. Several of the villagers, who greeted him by his first name, happened to be standing outside the pub when he loaded her case into the trunk, and Kelly realised just how easy it was for information to spread through the place. It was another fine spring day and she enjoyed the short drive up to the Hall, along the tree-lined avenue that held no fears for her now. Mrs Banks met her and showed her to a room that was much larger than the one she'd had at the inn, but was equally attractive, if less feminine. There was a beautiful old four-poster bed that was so high it almost touched the ceiling, and was hung with heavy pale-blue damask. All the furniture was old and lovingly polished, but there was also the modern luxury of thick fitted carpet, central heating, and a shower-room converted from what must have been a dressing-room, that opened off the bedroom. The windows were latticed, small diamond-shaped panes of old glass that reflected the light in muted colours. Kelly pushed open one of the windows and leaned out over the stone sill, revelling in her surroundings. Her room was at the back of the house and looked out over the landscaped gardens of rockeries, flowerbeds and lawns thick with daffodils and tulips, but screened by many trees that had not yet come into leaf. It was a perfect setting for the house, and it smelt so fresh and clean. Idyllic.

She turned to Mrs Banks with a smile of delight. 'Isn't it beautiful here? Don't you just adore it?'

The older woman smiled at her enthusiasm. 'Oh, yes, it's very pretty,' she said good-naturedly.

'I expect you're used to it. Have you always lived in Ashdon Magna?'

'No, we only came to work here after Mr Charles had his accident. Before that we lived the other side of Oxford,' she told Kelly, speaking as if the town was a thousand miles away.

'Was that before Byron came to live here?' Kelly enquired casually, reckoning that if anyone knew about the family scandals it would be the live-in housekeeper.

'No, I think he'd been here some time before we came,' Mrs Banks answered. 'I was a nurse once, you see, so I came to look after Mr Charles when he came out of hospital, as much as to take care of the house.'

The housekeeper was willing to chat, but mostly asked questions of Kelly, tut-tutting with ready sympathy when she heard about her parents. 'I thought you looked thin and pale,' she remarked.

'We'll have to feed you up and put some roses in your cheeks.'

Kelly smiled at the expression. Mrs Banks left her in order to go and prepare lunch, and Kelly unpacked her things, hanging them in the tall Empire-style wardrobe. Afterwards she explored the rooms downstairs, wandering into a large dining-room with a long refectory table and display cabinets on the walls full of old china and silver, and one with nothing but silver cups and plates, each inscribed and obviously won as sporting prizes. There were portraits round the walls, too, as well as paintings. Over the big stone fireplace there was a modern-looking portrait of a young man whom Kelly recognised as Cousin Charles, and to its left a companion portrait of a young woman that she guessed must have been his wife. And, strangely, on the other side of Charles's portrait there was a space, as if another picture had hung there and been taken down. There was even a faint mark of discoloration on the painted wall where it had hung. Perhaps it had been taken down to be cleaned, Kelly thought idly. She was more interested in looking at some photographs, but they were all very old ones in sepia and grey, and there was no one who looked even remotely similar in looks or age to herself.

She found a library too, in which the sun shone on to glass-fronted cases full of richly bound books with gold titles. And piled on to a lower shelf she found old account books written in beautiful copperplate with dates in the seventeen hundred's. Kelly somehow dragged herself away from such treasure, the knowledge that her ancestors had been a part of all this filling her with wonder, and went to find Charles Thorne.

He was in his sanctum, and smiled and greeted her warmly. The curtains were open now and Kelly could see through the french windows out to a terrace with steps that led down to the garden. 'This is such a beautiful place,' Kelly enthused. 'You must love it here.'

His lips curled with amusement and pleasure. 'Why, yes, I do. But then I've lived here all my life, so I've got used to it.'

'But it's such an old house. Do you know all its history? Would you tell me?'

It seemed she had touched on a subject close to his heart, for he immediately launched into a detailed history of the house which involved going in his electric wheelchair from room to room as he showed her the documents giving the Thornes the lordship of the manor that were kept in the library, or pointing out the portraits of the various people he spoke of. 'And that,' he told her eventually, pointing to the portrait of an elderly gentleman in Edwardian-style clothes, 'is my great-grandfather and your great-great-grandfather. Beside him is his wife, and the painting on the other side is of his three children who would be my grandfather, your great-grandfather, and great-aunt Lilian.'

'Wow.' Kelly looked up at the paintings in awe. 'Wow,' she said again, quite overwhelmed.

Charles smiled and, as a dozen clocks in the house began to chime, said, 'Why. it's lunch time already. Let's go and eat, shall we?' He led the way back to his own room, the wheelchair giving out a gentle purring sound from its motor. He offered her an aperitif and poured it for her himself today. A table had been set by the window, but set for only two.

'I thought we might eat in here,' Charles told

her as he followed her glance. 'So much more comfortable than the dining-room.'

'Won't Byron be joining us?' Kelly couldn't resist asking.

'No, he's working today. He has an office in Gloucester. He's a solicitor, you know.'

'A solicitor?'

'A lawyer. He works there two or three days a week, and spends the rest of the time running the estate.'

Their lunch was a happy meal, served by Mrs Banks. Mr Thorne didn't eat very much but he talked quite a lot, telling her about the birds that came to a bird-table just outside the window to feed. And he drew her out to talk more about herself, although she insisted that there wasn't much to tell. 'I just went to school, then on to college for a couple of years, and from there to a bank in the city. I had intended to make a career in banking but . . .' Her eyes dropped. 'Since Mom and Pop were killed I've found it difficult to concentrate on anything.'

'So you decided to have a holiday. The best thing you could do. Get right away for a while and see new places, new people.'

His voice was encouraging, just what Kelly needed and she nodded eagerly. 'That's what I thought.' But then her mouth twisted a little wryly. 'But perhaps I shouldn't have just turned up here. I should have written first.'

'I thought you did write.'

'Only to tell you about the accident. I didn't say that I was coming because I hadn't decided to then. And when I didn't get any reply I figured that you must have moved house, so I really came just to make enquiries about you. But they told me at the

Horn that you still lived here, so . . .' She shrugged. 'So I came on up, anyway.'

She didn't ask a question, but there was one in her tone, and Charles Thorne picked it up at once. 'You're wondering why Byron didn't show me your letter or reply to it. He had his reasons, Kelly. And to him they are very good and valid reasons. But please believe that if I had seen your letter I would have written to you at once and asked you to come here.'

'Thank you,' Kelly looked into his sincere eyes and nodded. 'I do believe it.'

'And do you have any future plans? Any boy-friend in Canada waiting for you?'

Kelly smiled and shook her head. 'No one special.'

'But I'm quite sure that a girl as pretty as you doesn't want for boyfriends?'

'Well, no,' Kelly admitted with rather a sad smile. 'But not lately.'

'You know,' Mr Thorne said with rough gentle-ness, 'I've found from my own experience that it doesn't do to hug your grief to you and shut other people out. Sorrow is much like happiness, and is better off if it's shared.'

She nodded and blinked back a sudden tear, overwhelmed by his understanding. 'You—you've lost your wife, too, haven't you?' she asked as she tried to control her emotions.

'Yes, but that was many years ago. Time tends to dull the pain, thankfully.' But then his face grew sombre. 'Or at least, some pain. Not all.'

Kelly thought he was talking about his physical pain and gave him a sympathetic look. To change the subject she said, 'I notice that you seem to have the portraits arranged in family groups.'

'Yes, they've always been put up that way, it gives them a better chronological sense, I think.'

'But in the dining-room,' Kelly pursued, 'there's a portrait of you and one of a lady who I guess was your wife, and just an empty space on the other side. Don't you have any children?'

It was an innocent enough question, and there was no way Kelly could have foreseen Charles's reaction to it. He went first white and then his face suffused with angry colour. 'No,' he said harshly. 'I have no children now.'

'Oh, I—I'm sorry.' Kelly looked at him in distress, thinking that his child must have died, that this was the subject Byron had been afraid she'd bring up and upset her cousin. But why hadn't Byron told her? Why had he just let her fall into it like this? Angry indignation filled Kelly at his under-handedness. But it was strange; she wouldn't have suspected Byron of such a cheap trick. Surely he would think it beneath him? But one thing was for sure, she thought grimly, she was going to have this out with Byron the first moment she saw him!

CHAPTER THREE

IT WAS such a lovely day that, after lunch, Kelly and
Charles Thorne put on their coats and went into the
garden. A special ramp had been built over part of
the steps and the paths had been widened to take his
wheelchair, so her host had no difficulty in going
round it. The garden was obviously one of his chief
interests, and Charles pointed out the trees and
shrubs and few flowers that were out, telling her
their names and asking her if they grew in Canada.
Kelly had to admit to ignorance on most of them;
having lived most of her life in a city apartment, she
knew very little about gardening.

Her cousin was shocked at her not having a
garden. 'The most wonderful thing in the world,' he
told her, 'is to plant a garden and watch it grow.'

They spent a pleasant couple of hours wandering
around, the time flying by as Kelly walked alongside
the wheelchair. She was careful not to speak of
anything personal again, and her cousin Charles
became quite cheerful, often smiling at her and a
couple of times touching her hand. He invited her to
pick some narcissi to take back to the house, and
Kelly gathered a large bunch of the delicate yellow
flowers, giving one to Charles to put in his
buttonhole, which made him chuckle. And they
were laughing in pleasant companionship, Kelly
holding the flowers close to her face so that she could
smell the scent, when Byron came striding across

the lawn and pushed aside some fronds of weeping willow to find them.

Kelly turned and felt as if the sun had gone out of the day when she saw his stony face.

'Good afternoon,' he said shortly, nodding curtly to her and then turning to Charles. 'Aren't you feeling cold having been out here so long? Mrs Banks said you've been in the garden for nearly two hours.'

Kelly immediately felt guilty, but then realised that Charles would have told her if he'd wanted to go in. It was Byron who *wanted* her to feel guilty.

'Not at all,' Charles said firmly. 'We've been having a most pleasant afternoon.'

'Nevertheless, I think it would be a good idea if you went in now.'

Byron didn't make any attempt to take hold of the chair, but Charles looked at him challengingly. 'Would it, indeed?'

For the first time since she'd met him yesterday, a trace of humour came into Byron's face and, contrary to her expectations, there was no clash of wills between the two men. 'I see you're improving rapidly,' Byron remarked. 'Almost back to your old self again.'

Charles smiled. 'I'm becoming pig-headed again, you mean.'

'You said it, not me.'

That brought a laugh to Charles's face which was pleasant to see, but he said, 'You're right, of course, it's about time we went in. But it's been a most enjoyable afternoon. Most enjoyable.' And he smiled at Kelly. 'Thanks to you, my dear.'

Byron gave Kelly a frowning glance, but encountered such an angry stare in return that his eyebrows rose in surprise. He didn't say anything though, merely turning to walk back through the garden, with Charles steering the chair beside him. Kelly followed, only half listening as they began to talk of some business matter. They were both strong-willed men, she thought, and it was possible that his illness had made Charles cantankerous, but it was evident that Byron knew exactly how to handle him. And he certainly didn't seem to defer to him as an employer, but spoke to him as if they were on equal terms.

They reached the french doors and Charles went inside while Byron stood politely waiting for her to go ahead of him. Kelly walked slowly forward, her eyes still antagonistic. But Byron was looking at the flowers she carried and there was a bleak look in his dark eyes. She paused and he lifted his head. For a moment their eyes held, but then his mouth twisted and he lifted his hand to gesture at her jacket. 'The sap is staining your clothes,' he said shortly.

Kelly glanced down. 'I'll go and put them in water,' she said quickly. But as she went past him she was sure that it had been some memory that made him look so bleak.

Mrs Banks wasn't in the kitchen, but there was a sound of a vacuum cleaner upstairs so Kelly went up to look for her. She found her in a bedroom at the front of the house. 'Hi. Could you tell me where I can find a vase to put these in?' Kelly moved forward into the room as she spoke, and gave a little gasp of delight as she looked around her at the lace-hung bed, the floral draped curtains and the pretty dressing-table. 'What a beautiful room!'

'Yes, it's pretty, isn't it?' Mrs Banks turned off the cleaner. 'I'll take them for you, shall I? Oh, dear, they've dripped on to your jacket. That's the worst of narcissi. Does it wash, do you know?'

'Well, yes, I guess so, but—please, you don't have to bother. I'll just give it to the cleaning company when they call and . . .'

'I'm afraid you have to take things to the cleaners here, but if it will wash I can do it for you straight away.'

So Kelly handed her the jacket, saying, 'Whose is this room? It's very feminine.'

'Oh, nobody uses it. Usually it's kept locked, but I clean it out regularly. Mr Byron likes me to do it rather than the daily cleaning woman. Would you like the flowers in your bedroom? I won't be a moment, then I'll bring them up.'

The housekeeper went away, but Kelly lingered to look round. It didn't look like a neat guest-room, but as if someone was using it. It had evidently been the room of someone who loved horses, for there was a whole collection of models of them on shelves and window-sills. There was a bookcase full of novels too, and pots of creams and make-up on the dressing-table with its frilled skirt. In fact, the room looked as if its owner had merely gone away for a few days and would soon be back to take up residence again.

The sun reflected off the glass of a picture on the wall, and Kelly moved to one side to see it better. It was the portrait of a young girl, perhaps a few years younger than herself, but with the same dark hair and fine-boned features.

As she looked at it there was a sound in the doorway and then Byron strode in, his face taut with anger. 'What the hell are you doing in here?' he demanded fiercely.

'Taken aback by his anger, Kelly said defensively,

'I came to find Mrs Banks,' and indicated the vacuum cleaner.

'You shouldn't be here,' Byron said shortly, and held the door for her to leave.

But by that time Kelly had remembered that *she* was the one who should be angry. Lifting her chin, she said, 'Now, just you wait a minute. Why didn't you tell me that Cousin Charles had a child who died? You warned me not to upset him and yet you let me blunder into that! I call that real sneaky to not tell me and . . .'

Byron stepped into the room, shut the door, and caught her gesticulating hand. 'What are you saying?'

'You already know,' Kelly retorted. 'I think it was a downright mean trick not to tell me that Cousin Charles's daughter had died.'

His brows frowning, Byron said, 'Is that what he said to you—that she'd died?'

'Yes. Well, no, not exactly. But it's perfectly obvious. This was her room, wasn't it?'

But Byron gave her wrist an impatient shake. 'Tell me exactly what Charles said,' he ordered brusquely.

Kelly gave him a resentful glance, but he was so insistent that she thought back and said, 'He said that he had no child *now*. Yes, those were his exact words. But why do you want to know? What difference does it make? I still think you're a rat for not . . .'

But Byron had released her wrist and stepped away from her. 'She's not dead,' he said shortly.

'Not?' Kelly stared at him. 'But I don't understand. Why did he say that he had no child?'

Moodily Byron walked over to look at the picture

on the wall. He didn't answer for a moment, then gave an exasperated sort of sigh, the exasperation evidently pointed at Kelly, because he said curtly, 'I suppose you'd better know. You're nothing if not persistent, so you're bound to find out some time. Elaine isn't dead. She . . .'

'Elaine?' Kelly broke in. 'You mean the girl you mistook me for?' Quickly she went to look at the picture again, then at herself in the dressing-table mirror, and caught her breath. Yes, she could see it now. There *was* a resemblance, but only in colouring and the shape of the face, the features weren't very similar. 'What happened to her?' she asked, her voice loaded with curiosity.

'She ran away,' Byron said abruptly. 'She wasn't—content with the life she had here, so she ran away over two years ago.'

'And has she disappeared? Hasn't she ever been heard of again?' Kelly asked, ready to be shocked.

Byron gave a harsh kind of laugh. 'No, she did go to see her father when he was in hospital.'

'She wanted to come back?'

'Oh, no, that was the last thing she wanted.' His mouth had twisted, making Kelly remember what an emotional shock it had been to him when he'd mistaken her for Elaine.

'Have you seen her since?' she asked a little awkwardly.

His features immediately drew into a taut mask. 'No,' he said coldly. 'I haven't.'

After one look at his face Kelly decided it would be wiser not to question him any more on that point, but she said, 'I still don't understand why Cousin Charles said that he had no child. Surely he hopes that Elaine will come back one day?'

'No. One thing you'll learn about Charles is that
he is unforgiving in his anger.' He swung round, as
if deliberately turning his back on the portrait. 'As
far as he's concerned, Elaine has deserted him, left
him to make her own life. He wants nothing more to
do with her. That's why he had her portrait taken up
here and the room locked. He never even talks about
her.'

'But Mrs Banks was cleaning in here.'

'Oh, I have her do that. Just in case.'

The bleak look again came into his eyes, but Kelly
missed it as she turned on him angrily. 'Why didn't
you tell me this before? Didn't you realise that I
might ask about his children? I could so easily have
upset him badly.'

'Perhaps I should have.' Byron retorted. 'But it's
a very personal matter to this family.'

'You're darn right you should have,' Kelly
replied heatedly. 'And it may have escaped your
notice, but I happen to be a member of this family,
too. More so than you are, if it comes to that!'

A belligerent look came into Byron's dark eyes.
'You're taking rather a lot on yourself, aren't you?'

'You should have told me,' Kelly retorted
obstinately.

Byron glowered at her, but said, 'If you must
know, I wasn't particularly afraid that you would
upset Charles by talking about Elaine. He can
handle that. He just shuts people out until they get
the message. But I was afraid that he would see how
strongly you resemble her and that he might make
the same mistake I did. I was afraid that it would be
a bad shock for him.'

As it was for you, Kelly thought, but she didn't
say anything, just waited until he'd finished.

'But obviously he took it in his stride,' Byron went on. 'When I saw him at breakfast this morning, he said that he had noticed a family resemblance, nothing more.'

'So where does that leave me?' Kelly demanded. 'Do I talk about Elaine or not?'

'Definitely not. Forget you ever heard of her. Charles certainly won't mention her name. In fact, I'm surprised that he even asked you to stay here when looking at you must be a constant reminder to him.'

'You're very protective towards him,' Kelly remarked.

Byron shrugged. 'He's very vulnerable at the moment.'

She looked at him thoughtfully, wondering what reason he had to guard his cousin. Was it because he pitied him? Or was it family feeling? Whatever it was it seemed that Byron had taken on a whole lot more than just the care of the estate. He walked to the door again, but Kelly turned back to the portrait.

'How old is she?'

'That portrait was painted for her eighteenth birthday. But she will be almost twenty-one now.'

'Nearly the same age as me,' Kelly commented. She glanced at Byron. 'Did you know her, then?'

'I've always known her,' he answered shortly. 'All her life.'

'And did you get on well with her?'

He gave a grating kind of laugh, a laugh so harsh, so mirthless that it almost frightened her. 'I thought so—once.'

The way he said it reminded Kelly of when Charles Thorne had said he had no child—now. She wondered if Byron, too, could be unrelenting in his anger. But no, he had had the room cleaned, just in case Elaine came back. But her running away must have been a terrible shock for him, too, if he thought he'd been close to Elaine.

Kelly was about to ask him another question, but they heard footsteps in the corridor and Byron opened the door. Mrs Banks came in and smiled at her. 'I've put the flowers in your room, miss. And your jacket should be as good as new.'

'Thank you,' Kelly said, but her eyes were on Byron as he went out of the room and down the corridor to a door farther along.

They had an early dinner that evening, the three of them, served in the dining-room, a magnificent room in the oldest part of the house, that rose to a beautifully curved wooden ceiling that Mr Thorne told her was called a hammer beam roof. The room was so large and there were so many old portraits on the walls that Kelly felt almost as if she was in a church and should speak in a hushed voice. No wonder her host hadn't wanted to have lunch in here. But a bright log fire was burning in the stone fireplace, the wood giving off a pleasant rising smell as it sparked and crackled.

Byron and Charles obviously were used to the room and didn't find it at all overpowering. The latter guided his wheelchair to the head of the refectory table and motioned Kelly to sit on his right. Byron came to sit opposite her, for which she was grateful; she had imagined they might all be spaced down the length of the table and have to shout at one another all through the meal.

Seeing the look of relief on her face, Charles gave a small chuckle. 'Don't worry, Kelly, we're not that old-fashioned.' He poured her a glass of wine. 'I'd like your opinion of this. Do you know much about wine?'

'A little. We mostly had imported French wines at home.'

'Well, this is an English wine, made at our new vineyard, that has only recently started bottling enough to make it a commercial venture.'

'Your own vineyard?' Kelly asked, her eyes widening.

'Oh, a very small one. Only a few acres. Well, what do you think?'

'It's fine. I like it.'

She asked him about the vineyard and Byron joined in the conversation, showing no outward signs of constraint or antagonism. He was attentive and polite, asking if the food was to her taste, and refilling her wineglass. He made sure that she wasn't left out of the conversation, adeptly turning it to include her again if they got on to people or places she knew nothing about. In fact, if Kelly hadn't known full well that he didn't want her there, it would have been easy to think that he was treating her as a welcome guest. But perhaps that could be put down to his innate good manners.

Kelly studied Byron covertly as she ate and talked. He seemed very knowledgeable, able to converse on any subject, although he admitted that he had never been to Canada. He smiled sometimes but didn't laugh very often, and when he did it lacked genuine spontaneity, almost as if he didn't find life particularly amusing. Kelly found herself intrigued. Byron began to be an enigma that she wanted to solve. And the more she saw him the more attractive he became. His physical impact she had felt already. She had met handsome men before, perhaps even better-looking by modern-day standards; but there was something about Byron that drew her. She tried to figure out what it was. Perhaps his foreignness, she thought. Or his sophistication and self-assurance. Or perhaps the withdrawn, keep-your-distance air that made you think him emotionless—unless you'd seen the reverse side of the coin as Kelly had the first time they'd met. Or maybe, she thought as her hand happened to touch his, maybe it's just good old-fashioned male magnetism, after all.

Byron glanced up and her eyes met his for a moment. His face sharpened a little, but then he looked away and they both went on talking as if nothing had happened. Not that anything had, of course, but Kelly knew by the tingle down her spine that their relationship had subtly altered and was now on a far more personal level.

Charles Thorne asked how she had liked the Horn of Plenty, and went on to give her a potted history of the village, promising to take her to see the little local history museum. Kelly listened with interest, but was aware of Byron's eyes on her, and she wondered if he was studying her as intently as she had him.

When they'd finished the meal Byron went over to the sideboard for a decanter of port. As he was about to pour it, Kelly said hesitantly, 'Say, I read in a book that in England all the women have to leave the dining-room while the men drink their port. Shall I go and sit in the drawing-room?'

To her surprise, both men laughed. 'I'd like to know what authors you've been reading,' Charles remarked with a smile. 'I'm reliably informed that leaving men to their port went out with the Dark Ages.'

Kelly didn't have to wonder who his source of

information was. It seemed that his daughter's spirit still had an effect on Charles, even if he didn't realise it. 'Oh, good,' Kelly said, 'I've had enough of sitting alone.'

Byron gave her a quick, contemplative glance and said. 'Maybe you'd like to join us in a glass of port, then?'

As Kelly sipped hers, she nodded towards the trophy cabinet and said. 'You have so many cups and things. What did you win them for?' And she got up to have a closer look.

'They're mostly polo trophies,' Charles told her. 'I used to play quite a lot when I was younger. In fact, I think you'll find they're nearly all something to do with horses.'

There were a great many large silver cups and plates which all bore Charles's name and dated backwards from fifteen years ago. But there was a group of much smaller and less pretentious cups too, and when Kelly peered closely at them, she saw they were engraved with the name Elaine Thorne and covered about six years. So not everything of Elaine's had been thrown away, then. Had Charles overlooked these—or had he been so proud of his daughter's winning them that he hadn't been able to bear throwing them away?

Turning back towards the men, Kelly found Byron watching her narrowly, but she just said casually, 'I don't see any of your trophies there, Byron. Don't you play polo?'

His mouth twisted a little. 'I'm afraid I haven't the time. Polo is a team game and calls for a bigger commitment than I can give.'

He spoke quite matter of factly, but it was almost as if they were having another, silent conversation. He had known Elaine's trophies were there and his eyes had challenged her to mention them, and when she had not he had registered approval. And Kelly found that she rather liked his approval, it gave her heart a feeling of warmth that it hadn't had since her parents had been killed. She came back to the table and took her place, but felt more at ease now, as if Byron's silent resentment had faded.

They talked about polo for a while, which Kelly had never seen, Cousin Charles becoming quite animated as he recalled some good matches he had taken part in, but then he recollected his duties as host and suggested they go into the drawing room for coffee. The drawing-room, after the magnificence of the dining-room, was almost cosy in comparison, even though it was still very large. There were fireplaces at each end of the room, but only one had been lit, and Mrs Banks had left the coffee on a low table near the fire.

Charles asked her if she played chess, and when she said yes he challenged her to a game. Although perhaps 'challenged' was the wrong word; Kelly guessed that he had only done it to be polite and kind, and fully expected to have a rather boring quarter of an hour until he soundly beat her. Or perhaps he would let her win for a little, as she was his guest. But his eyebrows soon began to rise in pleased surprise, and after a while he turned to Byron with a chuckle and said, 'The girl really can play!'

'So I see.' Byron was standing nearby, watching the game as he drank his coffee. 'Who taught you?'

Kelly smiled. 'My father mostly, but my mother was pretty good too. They belonged to a chess club back in Canada and they took me along almost as soon as I could walk. I can't remember a time when I didn't play. And I used to practice against a computer, too.' She moved a piece on the board and grinned at her cousin. 'Checkmate, I think.'

'Good God, so it is!' Her vanquished opponent looked at her with respect. 'You must teach me how you did that.' He looked up at Byron. 'Did you realise what she was going to do?'

'Only towards the end,' Byron admitted. He gave her a sudden grin that made her heart lurch. 'And just how many trophies have you got for playing chess?'

She coloured a little, but covered it with a laugh. 'A few, I must admit.'

'More than a few, I should think,' Charles said. He backed away from the board. 'Here, Byron, you give her a game and see if you can do any better.'

Byron hooked up a chair to take his place, and this time there was a different kind of challenge in his eyes. He was forewarned, of course, and didn't make the mistake that Charles had of playing a simple game. He opened with a gambit move, but Kelly knew a great many of those and had no difficulty in countering it. The game became tense, Kelly finding that Byron was a worthy opponent who in no way underrated her skill. They sat opposite each other over the board, the firelight flickering on them as they fought their battle of brain and skill, while Cousin Charles looked on, almost as if he were an umpire waiting breathlessly to declare one of them the winner. And as the game wore on, to Kelly's heightened imagination, it seemed that they were playing for much more than the game. She began to feel that if she could win she would also be accepted here, become a part of the household at Ashdon Hall. Byron was clever, very clever, but he hadn't played against the experts Kelly had, as she proved when she at last sat back and said, 'My game, I think. There's nothing you can do to stop me now.'

Byron's lips twitched as he looked round the board,

then he nodded. 'Yes, you're right. There's no stopping you.' And his eyes came up to meet hers in a look that told her he *had* accepted her. Not fully, perhaps, but enough not to want to drive her away.

'Bravo!' Charles exclaimed. 'And to think that I used to be able to beat your father hollow when he came to stay.'

Kelly looked at him teasingly. 'Oh, Daddy was very kind; I expect he let you win as you were his host.'

Both men burst out laughing, but it was at Byron that Kelly looked. For the first time his laughter had been genuine and there was real amusement in his eyes. 'But Charles is your host,' he pointed out. 'Aren't you kind enough to let him win?'

'If I were a man, I probably would have done,' she retorted unthinkingly, pleased that she had made him laugh. 'But being a girl and young, I've learnt that I have to stand up and fight if I want to win against the older generation.' She said it about chess of course, but immediately the words were out of her mouth realised how they must sound. To her chagrin the laughter died from Byron's eyes and his face became withdrawn again, and Charles, too, wheeled his chair away. She wanted to apologise, to say that she hadn't meant anything by it, but how could she when Charles didn't know that Byron had told her about Elaine?

To cover her embarrassment, she stood up and said, 'May I go to the kitchen and make myself a milk drink? Perhaps you might like one, too?'

'Mrs Banks will have left everything ready,' Byron said coolly. 'If you'll tell me what you like, I'll go and make it for you.'

'Thanks, but if you'd just show me, I'd like to do it myself so that I don't have to bother you another time,' Kelly said firmly, and walked out to the kitchen.

As Byron had said, there were mugs left out on the central table, together with a saucepan and packets of Horlicks and cocoa. Kelly looked at them unseeingly for a moment, but then heard Byron come into the room behind her.

'Let me do it for you,' he offered.

'*No, I can manage.*' Kelly picked up the saucepan, swung round, and walked right into him.

Byron automatically put up his hands to steady her, and for a moment they stood very close, so that Kelly's nostrils were briefly filled with the frankly masculine aroma of musky aftershave. But then she jerked her head back and said fiercely, 'I didn't mean to upset Charles. It wasn't intentional. I just spoke without thinking.'

For a moment Byron's hands tightened on her arms, then he let go and stepped back. 'I know. It's all right, don't worry about it.'

He took the pan from her and went to the big fridge to take out a bottle of milk. Kelly looked at his broad back and then said, 'Wouldn't it be better if you told Charles that I know about his daughter? I wanted to apologise to him just now but I couldn't.'

'Better not, I think. Not at the moment, anyway. It will only cause both of you embarrassment if you keep apologising every time you make a slip.'

'So what am I supposed to do, guard my tongue the whole time?' Kelly asked protestingly.

An amused look came into Byron's eyes. 'Could you?'

Kelly grinned in return. 'I guess I might find it pretty difficult at that.'

'Quite honestly,' Byron admitted. 'I'm not sure what to do for the best. Either way it's going to be difficult for you, I'm afraid. But as Charles invited you

here, then I think he's going to have to realise that you
are likely to make the same kind of comments that
Elaine did. You're both about the same age and
presumably have the same kind of ideas about the
older generation,' he added in a dry tone.

'Is that why she ran away?' Kelly queried. 'Because
she wasn't allowed to lead a life of her own?'

Byron turned to put the pan of milk on the cooker.
'Why so interested?' he asked, and Kelly could feel the
chill in his voice.

'Just curiosity, I suppose.' She moved round the
table so that she could see his face and, as she'd
guessed, found it cold and withdrawn. But, even so,
she probed further by saying, 'And if I knew why she
ran away, I would know better what to say.'

'You think so, do you?'

'Don't you?'

Byron turned and poured the heated milk into two
of the mugs. 'Help yourself to whatever you want to
put in yours. Charles has Horlicks.'

'Aren't you having one?'

'No, I have to walk down to the stables and make
sure that everything's secure there before I turn in.'
He looked at her frowningly, her unanswered question
heavy in the air. 'I told you why Elaine left,' he said
shortly. 'She decided that she didn't want—what she
had here. She wanted a different kind of life.'

'But I don't understand why Charles won't even
talk about her. Surely if all she wanted . . .'

She broke off as Byron gave her a light but
admonitory tap on the nose. 'Kelly, just leave it, will
you?'

It was said as lightly, but there was a hardness in his
eyes that effectively warned her off. It was as if he had
put up a solid fence of 'No Trespassing' signs, shutting

her out from these private family matters. She
shrugged. 'OK. But don't go cold on me again if I slip
up.'

Immediately his mouth relaxed. 'Do I go cold on
you?'

'Like ice.' She shivered exaggeratedly. 'As a matter
of fact, you very seldom thaw.'

His eyes went swiftly to her face, saw that she was
serious, and frowned, evidently surprised at her
remark. 'I'm sorry,' he said rather stiltedly. 'I hadn't
meant to be an—ogre.'

'An ogre!' Kelly laughed. 'Oh, I might have
described you as many things, but not an ogre.'

'Oh, really? What things?' he challenged.

But Kelly refused to be drawn. 'Maybe I'll tell you
when I know you better,' she told him with a hint of
provocativeness in her voice that she didn't know was
there.

Byron's lips twitched. 'I shall hold you to that. Will
you take Charles's drink in for him?' He held the door
from the kitchen for her and went to put on an anorak
from the cloak cupboard. 'Goodnight, Kelly.'

'Goodnight,' She watched him as he let himself out
of the front door, and stood for a moment lost in
thought. She wondered why he had built that wall of
ice around himself, what hurt he'd taken to make him
so withdrawn. It must have been pretty serious, and
usually when a man was seriously hurt it was because
of a woman. And it seemed obvious that it must have
been Elaine. But it couldn't have been just her running
away and wanting to be independent. It had to be far
more than that, or Charles wouldn't have reacted so
harshly, surely? Intriguing, Kelly mused. And now,
with Byron, it was becoming important too.

A sound from the drawing-room made her belatedly

remember that the drinks were growing cold, so she tore her mind from the puzzle and quickly went on her way.

It felt strange lying in the big four-poster bed that night, like something out of history. Kelly kept the light on for a while and started to read a book, but soon heard footsteps go by in the corridor and realised that Byron was walking past to his room. That felt strange, too. She gave up trying to read and lay back, thinking how her life had changed recently. A couple of months ago she didn't know that Charles Thorne existed, and now here she was, a guest in his house. And two days ago she hadn't known that Byron existed either. And now—now she just couldn't get him out of her mind. Not, she decided, as she fell asleep, that she *wanted* to get him out of her mind.

She ate breakfast alone the next morning. Her cousin, it seemed, always had breakfast in his room, and Byron had already left. When Charles Thorne came in he ordered the car to be brought round and they went out for a drive so that Kelly could see some of the interesting places in the area. She loved it, revelling in the picturesque stone villages, the soft and rolling landscape, the feeling of timelessness. They stopped often, Jim Banks pulling the car into the side of the road so that Charles could point out a particular spot to her and more often than not explain its history. He was very knowledgeable about the area, and Kelly wasn't at all surprised to hear that he was the chairman of the local history society.

At a couple of places where they stopped, Mr Banks helped him into his wheelchair and then came with them as they went round an old house that was open to the public, and then a museum and art gallery. It was a busy day and Kelly enjoyed it, but she went eagerly down to dinner that evening, only to be disappointed when she found that Byron had gone out straight from his office and wouldn't be joining them. She tried to hide the surge of disappointment, and told herself off for having felt it at all. After all, she'd only known him for a couple of days and she wasn't sure she even liked him. He was certainly different from most of the men she'd known back home. But, like him or not, when he came home around midnight that evening, she was still sitting in the drawing-room, curled up on a settee and reading a book on local history that her cousin had lent her.

'Hi,' she greeted him.

Byron's eyebrows had risen at the sight of her. 'Not sleepy?'

'No.' She closed the book and put it aside.

He crossed to a drinks tray on the sideboard. 'Want one?'

'Please. Gin and tonic.'

He poured them out and brought one over to her, his eyes running over her as she straightened her legs. 'Had a good day?'

'Great. Cousin Charles took me all around.' She saw his brows flicker and said quickly, 'Don't worry, though; I made sure he didn't get too tired.'

Byron gave a crooked smile. 'Do you do that often?'

'Do what?'

'Read people's minds?'

She laughed. 'It was pretty obvious that you'd immediately think I'd overtired him.'

'Well, I certainly mustn't become obvious, must I?' he said with cynical emphasis. He finished his drink and walked to the door, then hesitated. 'I'm going to check on the horses; would you like to come with me?'

Kelly got quickly to her feet. 'Of course.'

It was companionable walking through the darkness together, and it felt good to stride along beside him the short distance to the stables. They were situated in a walled enclosure, reached through an archway with a bell-tower on top. All built from the local stone, of course, and weathered by time into soft rounded shapes. There were six horses in the stables; the big black one that Byron had been riding that first day, a hunter, three that he said were mares, and a darling foal that was only about six months old and stood in a stall with his mother.

Kelly was rather nervous of the big horses but she loved the foal. 'What's his name?' she asked delightedly as she stroked its soft, velvety nose.

'Callisto, after the mythical nymph.'

'He's gorgeous. Are you going to keep him?'

'For a while. Then he'll be sold to be broken and used for riding.'

'Who looks after them?'

'A woman who lives in the village, Daisy Pickman. She comes up every day and puts them out in the paddock and generally takes care of them. And I ride whenever I can, of course.'

He went up to each of the horses in turn, stroking them, saying a few words as he did so. He was very gentle, his long, sensitive hands caressing each animal as it came up to greet him. Kelly stood back, watching, and felt a silly lump come into her throat as she saw this other, very tender facet of his character. She watched his hands stroking one of the mares, and wondered if he handled women like that, caressing them so skilfully that they moaned in pleasure, much as the horses whickered theirs.

Byron turned to leave and Kelly was glad of the deep shadows that hid the blush that had come to her cheeks at her own thoughts. 'May I come and see them again?'

'Of course. Whenever you want.'

She found little to say on the walk back to the house, and immediately said goodnight and went quickly to her room. But tonight sleep was slow in coming because Kelly had realised with startling clarity that she could very easily fall in love with Byron. And that, she thought, might not be a very wise thing to do.

It was raining the next morning. Kelly heard it pattering against her window-panes and went to look out, then pushed the window wide, taking a deep sniff of the wet grass and earth. It smelt extremely rural. But it made her want to go out, so she put on jeans and a sweater and mac and went outside. It felt good to walk in the rain. It wasn't something she did much back home; usually she just jumped in the car and went from door to door. Even the bank where she worked had its own underground car park. But this was English rain. She did a whirling dance and lifted her head up to it, letting it fall on her face. She laughed happily, her grief fading now when there were so many new things to think about. Like Byron. Kelly leaned against a tree trunk and decided that maybe she would let herself fall in love with him—if that thing called basic chemistry gave her a choice.

Almost as if the elements were in accord with her mood, the rain stopped and the clouds gave way to watery sunshine. Kelly laughed aloud again and ran down to the stables to see the foal, feeling full of happiness and excitement, full of the joy of being young and alive on a wet morning like this—especially on a morning like this.

The stall doors were open and there was the clanking sound of a bucket from inside one of them. A middle-aged and rather large woman with greying hair was swilling down the floor, but looked up when Kelly said good morning. 'I'm staying at Ashdon Hall,' she explained. 'My name's Kelly Baxter.'

'Oh, yes, I heard about you from Mrs Banks. How d'you do? I'm Daisy Pickman.'

'I came to see Callisto. I met him last night.'

The older woman grinned. 'He's already out in the paddock with the others. Do you know where it is?' And, when Kelly shook her head, 'I'll show you then.'

She led the way out of the stable yard, with Kelly asking questions about the horses. 'You seem to know them well.' she remarked.

'Oh, yes, I've been here a long time.'

A thought occurred to Kelly and she said, 'You must have known Elaine, then, Mr Thorne's daughter?'

'Yes, indeed. She was a good rider. She'd have had a future in show-jumping if only she hadn't run away. It was a pity, a great pity. But then, I suppose she felt she had no other choice. But to run off at a time like that . . .' Daisy Pickman shook her head in disparagement.

'Like that? Like what?' Kelly ventured, agog with curiosity.

'Why don't you know? She ran away almost on the eve of her wedding day.'

'Really? Wow!' Kelly's eyes widened in shocked surprise. 'What a horrible thing to do. Who was she supposed to marry?'

It was the other woman's turn to look surprised. 'Why, Byron, of course!'

CHAPTER FOUR

KELLY came to a standstill and stared at Daisy Pickman, open-mouthed. 'You mean—you mean Elaine walked out on Byron the day before their wedding?' she demanded incredulously.

'Well, a few days before, certainly. Everything had to be cancelled and the presents sent back. But of course that paled into nothing because of Charles's accident.'

Daisy said it with a kind of relish, and Kelly realised she was a born gossip who would enjoy relating this scandal now that it was a part of history. Not a vicious person, rather one who took an intense interest in her fellow human beings, for there was a well of sympathy in her voice.

'Cousin Charles's accident happened about the same time?'

'Yes. The one caused the other, really.' They reached the paddock and Daisy settled comfortably against the fence, the horses forgotten. 'I can see I'd better start from the beginning. Well, now, did you know the estate is entailed—that means it's been left so that it will pass from Charles to Byron? You see, Charles's father got into financial difficulties some forty or fifty years ago. He invested a great deal of money in an overseas venture and lost the lot because of the war, the Second World War, that is. Well, Byron's grandfather came to his rescue, being a relation, and gave him a loan against the estate, a sort of mortgage, but the agreement was that if Charles

73

had no male heir the estate was to revert back to Byron's branch of the family.'

'But can they do that? What about Elaine?'

'Oh, yes, it was a binding agreement. But Charles obviously didn't want Elaine to lose the estate, even though he'd provided for her, so he made sure that Byron and Elaine knew each other from children. Everyone hoped they would marry, to tidy things up, expected them to, really. And I think Charles put too much pressure on Elaine.'

'You mean she was forced into it? And Byron, too?'

'Good heavens, no. Charles wouldn't have forced her. And Byron was nearly thirty, there was no forcing him to do anything he didn't want to. There never has been. No, it was more that it had been taken for granted ever since Elaine's mother died when she was only little. There was no son to take over, you see. But Charles loved his daughter and naturally wanted her to have the benefit of all that he'd worked for. And he was impatient. He wanted it all settled, to have them married and Byron living here permanently and helping with the estate. So he pushed Elaine into getting engaged when she was only eighteen, straight from school, and arranged the wedding for when she was nineteen, a few months later.'

'But what about Byron in all this?' Kelly queried. 'Did he just fall in with what they wanted?'

'Largely. I think he wanted to be settled in one place, too. But I'm sure that he would have waited if he'd thought that Elaine was at all unsure or unhappy.' Daisy turned and leaned back against the fence, squinting her eyes against the sun. 'But that was the point, you see, Elaine *was* happy at first. I suppose she enjoyed all the fuss and excitement, just as any young girl would. It was only as the wedding drew nearer that she began to realise that there might be more to life than getting married, especially so young.'

'Didn't she speak to Byron, tell him how she felt?'

Daisy shook her untidy grey head. 'Byron was away. He'd gone abroad somewhere and wasn't due back until just before the wedding. Which was a great pity. Elaine only had her father to turn to, and Charles is a stickler for keeping his word, and the family honour and all that. He told Elaine she'd promised to marry Byron on that day and she must do so. No two ways about it. So I suppose Elaine felt she had no choice but to run away. And that, of course, caused quite an upset.'

'I imagine it might.' Kelly looked at her and said almost reluctantly, 'What happened?'

'Elaine left a note, rather a hysterical one, from what I can gather. Said she couldn't go through with it, and all that dramatic kind of stuff. Anyway, Charles found the note and guessed that she'd gone to Gloucester to catch a train to London. He went dashing after her, furiously angry and determined to bring her back.' Daisy paused, adding more slowly, 'Unfortunately he was so angry that when he ran across the car park to the station, he ran behind a big van that was reversing. It knocked him down and crippled him.'

Her face pale, Kelly said, 'Oh, but that's dreadful!'

Daisy nodded. 'He was rushed into hospital and Byron came home to find that his bride had disappeared and he had Charles and the estate to look after.'

'But Elaine went to see Charles in hospital, didn't she? Why didn't she come home then?'

'Well, for one thing Charles refused to see her. I don't think he blamed her for what had happened to him, but he certainly blamed her for letting Byron and the family down. He thought it was cowardly and he couldn't forgive her for that. So that made it impossible for her to go home, and anyway I think by then she'd had a taste of independence and she wasn't ready to go back. This was a few weeks after the accident happened, you see; I don't think she found out at first.'

'How did Byron take it?' Kelly asked, already imagining how he must have felt.

'Byron?' Daisy said musingly. 'He just closed up like a clam. He didn't tell anyone how he felt, not then or since. He just cancelled the wedding and did everything he could for Charles. I don't even know if he tried to find Elaine—or whether he would have taken her back if he had. But he's different now from what he used to be, more aloof. He keeps himself to himself, if you know what I mean.'

Kelly did, she had experienced that wall of ice around Byron herself, but was it his pride or his feelings that had been hurt? She asked the last and what seemed to be the most important question. 'You said it was taken for granted that they would marry; did Byron just fall in with the family wishes, too—or was he in love with Elaine?'

Daisy didn't hesitate, but said straight away, 'Oh, he was in love with her, all right. You mustn't think that he'd been just sitting around waiting for her to grow up. Byron had had more than a few girlfriends in his time and got serious with a couple of them, from what I understand. And the estate was to be his anyway, so he didn't intend to marry her for that. No, he was going to marry Elaine because he wanted her.'

She came to an end and they both tacitly turned to look at the horses, but Kelly's thoughts were far away.

Charles's attitude was fully explained now, and it seemed that even time hadn't lessened his hardness towards his only daughter. And Byron? Kelly's heart was wrung at the thought of him coming home to face all that scandal and pain, the terrible blow to his pride. No wonder he was sometimes so harsh and bitter. And no wonder that he had lost control of himself when he'd mistaken her for Elaine. Kelly shivered, remembering his fury, and was glad that she wasn't the girl who'd betrayed him.

'Well, I must be off. I've a lot of shopping to do today.'

Daisy's voice broke into her thoughts, and Kelly said goodbye but stayed where she was. She remembered how Byron had given orders that Elaine's room be kept cleaned, just in case she came back. Did that mean he was still in love with her, that he would willingly marry her if she came home? A romantic thought, but not one that pleased Kelly very much. She would much, much rather that Byron had been heartfree, because it was going to be one hell of a fight to convince him that he could fall for somebody else. But then Kelly smiled softly to herself, remembering that she had never refused a challenge yet.

Most of the rest of the day she spent with Charles or wandering round the grounds, looking at the ancient hexagonal dovecote where once hundreds of birds had filled the air with their cooing, but only a few remained. She saw too the long, timber-framed barns that had been serving the estate for centuries, and the pillared granaries where hay was still stored. It gave Kelly an exhilarating feeling of being part of history, as if flying across the Atlantic had also carried her back in time, and she wondered in amazement how anyone could run away when they were a part of this place.

And even more amazed that anyone could run away from Byron.

He was home earlier that evening and found her in Charles's sanctum, giving him a chess lesson. 'Hey, that's cheating!' he exclaimed. 'If you teach Charles all the gambits you know, I'll never be able to beat him.'

Charles laughed. 'You shouldn't have come home so soon. But it wasn't for your benefit, it was for John's. That's John Merrivale,' he added to Kelly. 'An old friend who comes to visit me every Friday evening. And if I can remember those moves I should beat him tonight.'

They all laughed, the atmosphere friendly and relaxed, but as Kelly looked at Byron she remembered what she had been told that morning, and fancied that the lines around his mouth must be those of pain. She felt a sudden urge to kiss them away, and to have him laugh and smile and be happy.

'Kelly's seen hardly anything of England yet, Byron,' Charles was saying. 'Why don't you take her over to Oxford? You should get there in plenty of time to see the place before it gets dark. And you could have dinner there.'

'Hey, wait a minute,' Kelly protested.

But Byron turned to her and said, 'Would you like to go to Oxford?'

'Why, sure, but I can take a bus some time. You don't have to take . . .'

'That's settled, then,' Byron said smoothly. 'Why don't you go and change, and we'll leave in about half an hour?'

Kelly got to her feet. 'Thanks, but you really don't have to . . .' Her voice faded as Byron raised a rather mocking eyebrow, and she grinned. 'OK. Half an hour.' And she ran to change.

At first she wasn't sure what to wear, but Charles had mentioned dinner and she decided to dress for that and to make as much impact on Byron as possible. So she put on her most stunning outfit of a deep red dress with narrow shoulder-straps and swathed skirt, which also had a thin matching stole that went round her neck and hung casually down her back. The deep red suited her dark hair, which she drew off her face into a far more sophisticated style. That, along with make-up and high heels, and Kelly felt ready to hold her own against any girl in Oxford.

She went down to the drawing-room, where Byron was waiting, and was glad that she'd taken the trouble to dress up because he was wearing an evening-suit and bow-tie, a cummerbund at his waist, and he looked—just devastating.

When he turned and saw her, he seemed to be taken aback for a moment, but recovered quickly to say stiffly, 'Do you have a coat? It will probably be chilly this evening.'

Kelly picked up her jacket, but he took it from her and helped her to put it on. 'You seem surprised,' she remarked as they got into his car.

'Surprised?' Byron raised a dark brow.

'By the way I look.'

He smiled a little. 'Gave myself away, did I? Yes, I am, rather. You seem very sophisticated tonight.'

'I'm a city girl. 'I am sophisticated,' she said deliberately.

He threw her a quick, assessing glance at that, but made no comment as they drove away from the Hall. Kelly didn't know whether to be pleased or not; she'd certainly made an impact on him, but he hadn't reacted in the way she'd expected him to, in the way that other men she knew had done. But then, Byron wasn't like any other man she knew. Was it being jilted almost at the altar like that that had made him so—so unapproachable? It suddenly occurred to Kelly that his abrupt reaction to the way she looked might be because she had reminded him of Elaine again, and she felt chill inside. One way and another, she thought angrily, that girl has a lot to answer for.

'Have you read or heard much about Oxford?' Byron asked her.

'Everybody's heard of Oxford. It's the city of dreaming spires, isn't it? And the boat-race crew, of course. Did you go there—to university, I mean?' He nodded. 'I guess that makes you sophisticated too, then,' she remarked, determined to try and draw him out, to pierce the icy wall.

'Hardly. I'm just as vulnerable as anyone else.' He said it dismissively, obviously not finding the subject to his liking.

'But you must have been around,' Kelly persisted. 'Any man as old as you must have.'

He laughed at that. 'You think I'm that ancient, do you?'

'*No*. You know what I mean.'

'Yes, I suppose I do. As you say, a man of my age must have been around.'

Kelly looked at him with annoyance, realising that all his defences were up. 'Well, aren't you going to tell me about yourself?' she pursued stubbornly.

Byron gave her a quick glance. 'Why so interested?'

'Because I'm staying in the same house with you and I want to get to know you,' she answered exasperatedly. Because you're taking me out tonight and yet you're still almost a stranger. Because you're English and you've been to Oxford. Because you've lived here all your life and I'm only a visitor. Because . . .'

'Enough!' Byron laughed and held up a hand. 'All right, where do you want me to start?'

'Why not at the beginning? Where did you live before you came to Ashdon Hall? Do you have any other family? Are your parents still alive?'

'You certainly want to know everything, don't you? My family home is in Norfolk, that's over on the east coast of England. My father died some time ago and my mother married again. She lives in London most of the time now. And I have an elder brother and a sister, who are both married. My brother and his family have taken over the house in Norfolk, but I go back there quite often.'

'So you're the playboy of the family, huh?'

Byron grinned. 'That may have been true once, but I assure you I'm very staid and respectable now.'

'How dull,' she remarked with a mock British accent, which made him laugh again. 'But somehow I don't believe it.'

'Don't you?' They had stopped at a road junction and he was able to turn fully and look at her, a quirk of amusement round his mouth. 'How about you?' he countered.

'Oh, but you already know all about me.'

'I very much doubt it. I'm beginning to think you have hidden depths.'

Kelly rather liked that, but said, 'You were going to tell me what it was like at Oxford.'

'Mm? Oh, yes.' He started to tell her about his student days, and gradually, as he talked, recounting anecdotes that made her laugh and brought a reminiscent grin to his lips, Kelly felt him relax and the beginnings of a rapport build between them.

Oxford arrived all too quickly, but Kelly instantly fell in love with the old town of churches and colleges as Byron drove her round the city, pointing out all the places she'd heard of so often. It was a perfect time to see it as the sun was beginning to set, casting a rich golden glow over towers and spires, as magnificent now as they had been centuries ago when they were first built. Byron parked the car and he took her for a tour round the town, pointing out Tom Tower over the gateway to Christ Church, and another college farther along, built in the sixteenth century and named after its famous doorknocker.

'A doorknocker!' Kelly exclaimed in amazement. 'I don't believe it. You're kidding.'

'No, I'm not. It's called Brasenose College, from the brazen-nose of the old knocker.'

He took her into his old college, spelt Magdalen but he pronounced it 'Maudlin', which left Kelly totally confused, and took her into the park that belonged to the college, where a herd of deer grazed contentedly in the middle of this big and busy city.

'It's unbelievable!' Kelly exclaimed. She looked round her wistfully at the beautiful old stone buildings. 'You're so lucky to have been educated in a place like this. It must give you a great feeling of—of belonging.'

'Why, yes, I suppose it does. I certainly enjoyed my time here and made a great many friends.'

He glanced at her, aware of the slight note of loneliness in her voice, and said bracingly, 'But you went to college, too, didn't you?' I expect you have the same feelings towards it.'

'I guess so. But it doesn't have . . .' she made a circling gesture with her hand ' . . . this air of timelessness. As if the place has always been here and always will. To have been educated here, to have been a tiny part of this, that must give you a sense of pride for the whole of your life.'

'Yes, I think it does,' Byron agreed. He smiled at her. 'You're a very . . .' He sought for a word. 'A very sensitive person.'

Her cheeks flushing a little with pleasure, Kelly shook her head. 'I'm just bug-eyed with wonder at it all.'

'I'm afraid it's getting too dark to see much more, all the colleges will be closed now.'

Going back into the town, they walked around for half an hour or so longer, because Kelly wanted to see the Bodleian Library that she'd read so much about. By then it was completely dark, so they drove along to a restaurant by the river where Byron had booked a table. Even the restaurant was unusual; it was a converted water-mill and still had the huge wooden paddle-wheel that had powered it in the main dining-room—cased in with glass now, but giving a great atmosphere to the place.

Here Byron was greeted by name as they went into the bar for an aperitif, and he nodded or spoke to several people he knew as they were later shown to their table.

'You know so many people,' Kelly remarked.

'Mostly people from university. And there's a branch of my law firm here too.'

'Your life is so different from mine.' She looked wistful for a moment. 'I wonder what my life would have been like if my parents hadn't emigrated to Canada.' Her eyes turned fully on him. 'I might have known you quite well.'

'Possibly, but not terribly likely. I seem to remember your father's family lived up in the north somewhere. Newcastle, I think.' He spoke as if it was very remote.

'How many thousands of miles away is that?'

Byron grinned. 'You north Americans all think that England is a small country, but it's just as much bother to go from one end to the other as it is in yours.'

She smiled back at him, glad that he seemed to be enjoying himself. He looked so different when he laughed, the lines of bitterness at the corners of his mouth smoothing out and his eyes creasing into an almost boyish grin. It made him look younger and almost carefree. And definitely more human and approachable.

Determined to make the evening a success and one he would remember, Kelly set out to keep him amused, at her most vital and sparkling as she encouraged him to talk more freely about his own life, and afterwards told him some hair-raising tales about the severities of the Canadian weather. One of them she embroidered shamelessly, and Byron's eyebrows rose incredulously. 'Good grief, that sounds impossible!'

'Well, of course it is. But it makes a good story, doesn't it?'

Realising that she'd been kidding him, he burst out laughing, making several diners turn to look at them. He picked up the wine-bottle to refill her glass, but then hesitated. 'Maybe you'd better not have any more, or else your stories will get taller yet.'

'As high as a Manhattan skyscraper,' she agreed, and when he groaned at the pun she smiled and reached out to cover his hand to make him fill her glass.

Byron laughed and for a few seconds resisted the pressure of her hand, so that she felt his strength and saw his muscles bunch beneath the smooth material of his jacket. But then he gave in and she took her hand away, feeling strangely confused and feminine.

They lingered over coffee, Byron in no great hurry to leave, but at last there was no excuse to stay and they went out into the foyer. The head waiter brought her jacket and would have put it on for her, but Byron took it from him. As he helped her with it his hand happened to touch her bare shoulder. A tremor ran through her and he said, 'Not cold already, are you?'

Kelly shook her head. 'No, I'm—I'm not cold,' she answered, her voice tight in her throat.

It was a beautifully clear night. Every star shone with glistening clarity, some so tiny that they looked like a cluster of diamonds. Kelly turned round, her neck craned, overcome by the enthralling magnificence of it all. She stumbled a little and Byron caught her. She leaned back on him and said dreamily, 'Isn't that the most beautiful sky?'

'Mm. Makes you feel small, doesn't it?' His breath moved her hair as he spoke and his hands came up to hold her arms and steady her. 'Small and transitory.'

'Yes,' Kelly agreed, sadly remembering her parents. 'But not unimportant. And it makes you realise that life is too short to waste.'

'Quite the philosopher,' Byron remarked with gentle mockery.

She turned and he let her go, but his arm stayed round her waist. 'But don't you agree? Surely it's criminal to let chances slip by—especially chances for happiness.'

'Perhaps. Have you let any chances go?'

'No, and I don't intend to,' she said firmly. She looked at him under her lashes and said, 'Have you?'

But that was probing a little deep, and Bryon's voice was grim as he said, 'Sometimes you don't recognise a chance when it comes along. And sometimes you think you have plenty of time to take it, but find that it's slipped from your grasp.'

'All the more reason to grab the next one,' Kelly told him forcefully, but then decided they were getting too serious and grabbed his hand. 'Come on, you haven't shown me the river yet. Now, I'm totally confused about this river. I always thought it was the Thames that went through Oxford, but in books it always seems to be called the Isis. And I thought Isis was some kind of Egyptian god!'

'I can see I shall have to educate you,' Byron told her, and began to explain as they walked along. Kelly moved nearer to listen and, as the grass was a little slippery, it seemed only natural that he should put his hand under her arm to steady her. She answered him and took it all in, but her heart was beating far too fast and she was filled with that heady kind of excitement that she was beginning to experience every time she was near him.

There was a path along by the river and they walked along under the trees for a little way, the moon turning the water to a rich silver stream. 'To think that this water flows all the way out to sea and maybe gets across the ocean to Canada,' Kelly said dreamily.

'I'm beginning to think you're a romantic,' Byron said with a grin.

'Is that a bad thing to be in England?' she asked warily.

He gave a delighted laugh but then said with mock seriousness, 'Indeed no, some of the most famous Englishmen have been romantics.'

'You're laughing at me,' she complained, and gave

him a playful punch on the chest. 'Are you romantic?'

He sobered suddenly, his mouth thinning. 'No,' he said shortly. 'It doesn't pay to be romantic.'

'Not even when you're in love?' she asked, keeping her tone light.

Byron gave a harsh laugh that was a world away from the genuine amusement he'd shown earlier. 'Especially when you're in love,' he answered bitterly.

Kelly looked at his set profile in the dim light; she would have liked to pursue it, to learn how he really felt, but she knew that it was too soon. And anyway she wanted him to remember the evening as an enjoyable one, so she laughed and said, 'OK, I'll just have to remember that when an Englishman is being romantic he definitely isn't serious. In Canada it's the opposite, you know. When a guy starts bringing you flowers and presents, you know he's hooked.'

He turned, his face relaxing. 'And have many men brought you presents?'

'Why, sure. I had this one neighbour who started giving me candy when I was eight.' She pulled a woeful face. 'But when I was ten he threw me over for a girl who had her own skateboard.'

As she'd hoped, that made Byron laugh again, but he said, 'Did you make that up?'

'Now would I?' Kelly demanded, her eyes opening wide with mock innocence.

'I'm beginning to think you might.' Byron gave her his full attention, his interest aroused. 'Maybe I was wrong about you,' he murmured.

'Wrong? In what way?'

'I didn't want you at Ashdon Hall,' he admitted bluntly.

'I know. You made it pretty plain.'

'Did I? I'm sorry.'

Kelly's heart began to thump a little as she said, 'Does that mean that you've changed your mind?'

Byron's eyes went to her face and he slowly nodded. 'Yes, I think it does.' Then his lips twitched. 'I think you'll be good company for Charles.'

He'd said it to tease her, she knew, but even so Kelly couldn't resist asking. 'And how about you?'

He grinned. 'Ah, now you disappoint me; that was a typically female question.'

'So? I'm female, aren't I? Or hadn't you noticed?'

It was a second or two before he answered, and then Byron said tightly, 'Yes, I've noticed.' He glanced at his watch. 'It's getting late. We'd better go.'

Well, at least she'd made some impression, Kelly thought as she let him lead her back to the car. On the way back she intentionally provoked him into an argument, finding out which side he took and deliberately taking the other. For a while they got quite heated, until Kelly finally admitted that she saw the force of his arguments. By that time they were back at Ashdon Hall and Byron was pulling up outside the house. He switched off the engine and turned to look at her, his lips curling in amusement, fully aware that it had been intentional. 'You know, Kelly, I've an idea that a man might get as mad as fire with you—but he'd never be bored!'

She laughed and got out of the car, waiting in the porch until he joined her. Lifting her head, she took a last glance at the stars.

'A perfect night,' Byron remarked as he, too, looked up at the sky.

'Yes.' She dropped her eyes to look at him. 'It

has been a perfect night. Thank you.' And stepping up to him, she kissed him lightly on the cheek.

He didn't flinch away, for which she was thankful, although his eyebrows did rise in surprise. Before he could say anything, she gave a shiver and said, 'Brrr, shall we go in?' Quickly he unlocked the door, and she merely said goodnight again and went straight up to her room.

Once there, Kelly undressed very slowly, reliving the evening, remembering how good it had felt to be with him. But the evening had proved that he was still very bitter, and that it was going to be a long and difficult task to break down the barriers that bitterness had built up. At least she'd made a start, Kelly thought with some satisfaction. Byron, she felt sure, was aware of her for herself now, and not just because she reminded him of Elaine. She knew that was important and that she must stress her own personality, but obviously there were going to be times when he was reminded of his ex-fiancée. She must learn what those times were and make sure she avoided them, Kelly resolved. But it was going to be difficult when she was such a complete stranger. Though maybe that had its advantages, too; there were so many places that she had never seen and that Byron would be able to show her. She began to fantasise about it and soon the fantasy became a dream.

From that evening Kelly really began to enjoy her stay at the Hall. She became relaxed and carefree, placing her grief for her parents into a private part of her heart where they would always remain. She still felt their loss just as greatly, and wished that she could share her life with them, but was sure that their love was still with her and that they would want her to enjoy her life to the full.

Cousin Charles's health continued to improve, and they often went out for drives together, with Jim Banks at the wheel as they explored the Cotswolds. They even went as far afield as Bristol and Bath. The latter city Kelly loved, with its Roman baths and beautiful Georgian crescents. It made her devour Jane Austen all over again. Byron came home one warm evening and found her still sitting out in the garden, deep in *Northanger Abbey*. She looked up as he came across to her and said excitedly, 'Do you know, the Assembly Rooms at Bath have hardly changed a bit since Jane Austen wrote about them? Wouldn't it have been wonderful to go to a ball there? Wouldn't it have been great?'

Byron smiled at her enthusiasm and sat down on the wooden seat beside her. 'I believe they still have dances there sometimes, although I don't know whether they're grand enough to be called balls.'

'They do? Wow!'

'Wow!' he echoed teasingly, mocking her accent.

She wrinkled her nose at him. 'Well, at least I don't sound like a news bulletin all the time.'

'Ouch!' He took a booklet from his pocket and tossed it on her lap. 'Here, a present for you.'

Kelly picked it up in pleased surprise. It was a guide and history of the town of Gloucester. Well, as a first gift it left much to be desired, but at least it proved that he'd been thinking about her. She lifted her eyebrows questioningly. 'Why, thanks, but . . .'

'It's where I have my office,' he reminded her. 'I thought you might like to ride in with me tomorrow and have a look round. And perhaps we might meet for lunch.'

'Yes,' Kelly accepted, her voice a little husky. 'I'd like that very much.'

It was a good day. She wheedled Byron into letting her drive his car part of the way, although he objected at first. 'Are you sure you can drive?'

'Of course I can. I've been able to since I was seventeen. It's just that everybody here drives on the wrong side of the road.'

'Oh, no. We've been travelling on the left-hand side since before Canada was even discovered. It's you who's wrong.'

'But Byron,' she said, 'How can we be wrong when we drive on the *right* side?'

'Oh, my God,' he groaned. 'Not a pun this early in the morning, please.' But he let her take over the wheel and, except for a couple of hair-raising moments when she started to go the wrong way round a roundabout, Kelly got along fine. But at the outskirts of Gloucester the traffic began to thicken and Byron took over to drive to the centre of town and drop her off. 'Bye. See you at one. Don't be late.'

She wasn't, although she'd been tempted to linger many times as she explored the old town with its many antique shops. They had lunch in an old pub near the centre of town. Kelly chose the traditional dish of steak and kidney pudding, and realised why the English were so well insulated against the cold and damp. She drew Byron out to talk about his law practice, and he mentioned that their receptionist would be leaving in a couple of months as she was moving away from the area.

'Really? Hey, maybe I could take her job,' Kelly suggested impulsively. Then caught her breath as she wondered if she'd gone too far.

But Byron merely said, 'Perhaps,' in a non-committal tone.

Kelly flushed. 'I guess you think that I ought to go before then. That I'll have outstayed my welcome.'

'Certainly not. You're doing wonders for Charles. I haven't seen him looking so animated since—since his accident. I'm sure that he wants you to stay as long as you like.'

'And you? Do you want me to stay, too?'

'Of course.'

'That's very polite of you,' she said coolly. 'But then you're always polite, even when you're being downright rude.'

He gave an incredulous gasp. 'Now what have I done?'

'You've just told me that you don't want me in your office,' Kelly retorted.

Tilting his head a little, Byron studied her face. 'I'm sure you'd make a perfectly good receptionist. But aren't you supposed to be on holiday? And I hardly think it would be fair to deprive Charles of your company when it gives him so much pleasure.'

Kelly nodded admiringly. 'Now that was clever. Flattering me and yet making me feel guilty at the same time. I'm beginning to think you have great experience at handling women, Byron.'

His eyes shadowed for a moment, but then he said, 'I suppose I have, when you consider the number of women clients who come to me for help.'

Their eyes met, Kelly's annoyed, Byron's quite bland, and they both knew that he had ducked the issue, but she let it go. After lunch she walked back to his office with him and arranged to meet him there at five. During the afternoon, Kelly forgot about history and old buildings. She indulged herself in an orgy of shopping, and was loaded down with parcels when she met him again.

'Why is it that women always go mad when they see dress shops?' he asked, but resignedly loaded all the parcels into the car.

Kelly had expected him to take her home, but instead he took her to the local theatre and afterwards to supper at a restaurant. 'That was fun,' she said dreamily as they got back into the car afterwards. 'Can we do this again some time?'

'You want to buy up a few more shops?'

She laughed and then gave an exclamation. 'Hey! Talking about shopping——' Kneeling up on the seat she leaned into the back to sort through her parcels. 'I bought you a present. Here it is.'

'Kelly, you shouldn't have.'

'Certainly I should. Here, take off your tie.' He protested but she turned, still kneeling on the seat, and did it for him. 'The guy in the shop said these were the latest thing. That every man of fashion should have one.' And she clipped a red silk bow-tie on to the front of his shirt.

'A red bow-tie!' Byron looked at himself in the driving mirror and burst out laughing. 'When do you expect me to wear it?'

'With your evening suit and red cummerbund,' Kelly answered indignantly. 'It will look great. Hey, stop laughing! It isn't that bad.' She leaned over to shake him, but got caught up with the handbrake and fell across him. 'Ouch! Will you stop it or I'll . . .'

But her words died in her throat as Byron's arms

closed round her, his face suddenly sobering. His eyes darkened in his taut face and his arms tightened as he gave a small, strangled sound and then bent to kiss her.

CHAPTER FIVE

IT DIDN'T last very long. Hardly had Kelly begun to respond and to raise her arms to put them round his neck, than Byron suddenly went rigid and drew back. 'I'm sorry,' he said shortly, in a voice full of anger at himself. 'That was a mistake.'

Biting her lips with chagrin, Kelly struggled back into her seat. 'I didn't think the tie was *that* bad,' she said after a moment, using flippancy in a desperate attempt to hide the hurt.

'It wasn't that! I . . .' Byron broke off and reached forward to hold the steering wheel, his knuckles showing white. 'We'd better get back.'

He went to switch on the engine, but Kelly reached out and stopped him. 'No, wait.' Licking lips gone suddenly dry, she said huskily, 'Don't you find me attractive, Byron?'

'Of course; you're a very attractive girl,' he answered woodenly.

'So why . . .' Her courage almost failed her at his stony face, but somehow Kelly managed to go on and say, 'So why did you stop kissing me?'

'It's really of no concern to you,' Byron said in a sharp voice that was intended to shut her up. 'I've already apolo——'

'Of course it's of concern to me,' she retorted. 'It was me you started to kiss. Remember? And I want to know why you stopped when it was getting interesting. I think I have a right to know.'

'Kelly, for heaven's sake! I . . .' He stopped with an exasperated sigh. 'It was wrong to take advantage of you. You're a guest and . . .'

'Oh, don't be so damn pompous!' Kelly broke in angrily. I didn't stop you, did I?' Her heart began to thump. 'Maybe I even quite liked the idea.'

He turned to stare at her. 'What are you saying?'

'That I like you. That I find you a very attractive man. That it might be—interesting to be kissed by you.'

She waited breathlessly, her eyes holding his. For a moment Byron looked almost amused at the way she'd phrased it, but then he turned moodily away. 'I'm flattered,' he said coldly.

'So you should be. I don't make a habit of telling men that.' She paused but he didn't say anything, so Kelly said, 'So tell me—why did you stop the way you did?'

'You wouldn't understand.'

'Try me.'

'It's a long story and one I don't feel like going into tonight,' he said in a brusque tone that was meant to finally close the conversation.

But Kelly could be equally stubborn. She looked at his set profile for a few moments, then said, 'In that case, I might as well tell you that I know about Elaine.'

He gave her a swift glance. 'Of course, I told you myself when . . .' His eyes narrowed when he saw the steady way she was returning his look. 'What do you know?'

'That you and she were engaged and she walked out on you.'

'Who told you?' he demanded angrily.

'Does it matter?'

'I suppose that means you're not going to tell me.'

He turned to glare at the darkness outside. 'I should have known that somebody would go gossiping to you. And I suppose you enjoyed listening to the scandal,' he added bitterly.

Picking her words, Kelly said. 'I was relieved to know why you went for me the way you did when you mistook me for Elaine that first day. As for the rest; well, it explains a lot of things. Why Charles was so angry—and why you're so bitter.'

'If you think I still care about her, you're mistaken,' Byron said, the harshness in his voice belying his words. 'She means nothing to me now. In fact,' he added as if it was absolutely necessary to convince her, 'I've been out with several girls since she left.'

'So why did you stop kissing me?' Kelly asked gently.

He gave her a sharp glance and then frowned. 'Maybe because I find you too darn attractive,' he muttered in a low, angry kind of growl that she only just caught.

Her heart beginning to race, she began. 'Byron, I . . .' But he reached forward and started the car, effectively putting an end to what was, for him, a very personal conversation.

They sat in rather a tense silence on the way back to the Hall, but when they reached it Kelly laughed. 'You've still got the bow-tie on,' she reminded him.

'Have I?' Byron put his hand up to his neck. Then he gave a rather wry grin. 'I don't think I thanked you for it, did I? It was very thoughtful of you.'

'Not at all,' she replied primly. 'Thank you for giving me such a pleasant day out.'

Realising that he was being teased, Byron gave a reluctant smile. 'I've an idea you're irrepressible.'

'Is that good or bad?' she asked warily.

His grin widened. 'Terrible. Come on, it's late. You'd better go in.'

He opened the door for her and left her to go in alone while he checked the stables. Kelly got into bed and listened for his tread in the corridor, but he was a long time. She lay with the curtains open, a shaft of moonlight silvering the room. She didn't feel very happy. Perhaps she should have been when Byron had kissed her. It must prove that he was at least aware of her, for God's sake! But it had been such a brief kiss before he'd drawn back. Because his shell had cracked for a moment and he was afraid of his own emotions? Or was it because his longing for Elaine was still so strong that he had momentarily thought of Kelly as the other girl and drawn back as soon as he realised. If it was the first reason, then that was wonderful, and Kelly could feel that she was really making some progress with him—even against his wishes. But if the latter? Kelly sighed. If he was still so much in love with his ex-fiancée, she didn't stand a chance. But one thing was for sure, she thought grimly; she wasn't going to be a substitute for someone else. If Byron ever kissed her again, it was going to be for herself.

The dawn light shining through the windows woke her early the next morning. It was a bright and beautiful day, the birds vying with one another to be the star of the dawn chorus. Kelly looked out and decided to go jogging as she'd often done round the park back home, often running several miles before breakfast. Also she'd bought a new designer tracksuit in Gloucester yesterday. It was a beautiful burnt orange colour, a tone that many women wouldn't be able to wear, but which suited her dark hair and tanned skin.

Letting herself out, Kelly loped easily down the drive and through the still quiet village, surprised not to see anyone else about. Maybe people didn't go in for jogging much in England. She came a different way back and entered the Hall grounds by a lane that led directly to the stables. Here Daisy Pickman was up and about, the horses, all except Byron's mount, already in the paddock.

'Hi,' Kelly greeted her.

'Morning. You're up and about early.'

'I needed some exercise. Too much good food and riding around in cars lately.'

'You ought to learn to ride,' Daisy recommended. 'That would give you plenty of exercise.'

Kelly looked at Daisy's ample size, and privately thought that she'd stick to jogging.

'Who ought to learn to ride?'

Byron's voice behind them made Kelly look quickly round. He was dressed in casual riding clothes, his hair still damp from the shower. His eyebrows rose at the sight of her, but his greeting was friendly enough. 'Hello. You're up early.'

'Why does everyone keep saying that?' she complained.

They both laughed and Daisy said. 'I suppose because the younger generation usually find it difficult to get out of bed. I know Elaine always did. I don't think she ever went riding before nine o'clock in the morning, even though she loved it so much.'

At the mention of Elaine's name, Kelly looked quickly at Byron and saw his brows draw into a frown. Surely he's not that sensitive? she thought in despair. But evidently he wasn't, because when Daisy left shortly afterwards he said, 'So that's where you heard all your gossip. I ought to have guessed.' Kelly was silent but he said, 'Daisy loves nothing better then discussing all the villagers' troubles.'

'I'm sure she doesn't do it out of malice,' Kelly protested. 'She seems genuinely interested.'

'Oh, she is. That's the trouble. And if you try to tell her off, she just doesn't understand. She thinks everyone is as sympathetic as she is.' With an abrupt change of mood he said, '*Do* you want to learn to ride?'

'No, thanks.'

'That sounded pretty definite.' he remarked in surprise.

'It is. Horses and I don't get on. At least, when I'm sitting on one's back we don't.' And she didn't intend to take up something that would make her look graceless and awkward compared to the expert Elaine, she thought forcefully.

Byron laughed. He seemed relaxed this morning, any tension from last night completely gone. 'Is that tracksuit for show or have you actually been jogging?'

'Certainly I have. All round the village and back, although that's only a short run compared to what I usually do.' She arched an eyebrow at him. 'Want to join me?'

But Byron gave a shudder and said, 'Maybe we'd better stick to our separate sports.' His eyes went over her. 'You look good this morning. That colour suits you.'

'Well, thank you, kind sir.'

He grinned and went into the stable to saddle up his horse, talking gently to the animal as he did so.

'Going far?' she asked.

'Down to the beech woods and out on to the open ground for a gallop.'

'Mind if I come with you part of the way?'

'Think you can keep up?' he asked in disbelief.

'I only said part of the way!'

So they set off together through the long acres of woodland, the man on his big black stallion and the girl running easily along beside him, the sun still low in the sky, shining through the trees and dappling them as they went. At first Byron kept the horse in check, but Kelly got in front of him, looked back and called out, 'Come on, what are you waiting for?'

Byron paused for a moment, an arrested expression in his dark eyes as he looked at her. She had taken off the top of her tracksuit and tied it round her waist. Under it she wore an athlete's vest that clung to her curvaceous figure and her hair had been blown into a mane of curls almost darker than the horse's. She looked young and vibrant and beautiful. Byron's mouth twisted for a moment, but then he gave an almost angry shake of his head, as if ridding himself of a painful thought that he totally rejected. Then he laughed and dug his heels into the horse's sides to catch her up again.

She left him at the end of the woods and watched as he loosened the reins and let the horse have its head. But after a quarter of a mile or so he turned and waved to her. Kelly felt good about that wave and even better about the smile that went with it; it made her self-confidence, never very down, soar again.

From that moment, Kelly was sure that Byron thought of her as individual and not a girl who reminded him of his ex-fiancée. That she might also sometimes make him regret what might have been didn't occur to her. She wasn't experienced enough to understand how such a blow to a man's pride could affect him. She only knew that she had to try to kill the bitterness that had taken such a hold on him. And gradually, as the days became weeks, the lines around

Byron's mouth smoothed out a little and he seemed much happier. He hurried home from the office now and they often went out together, sometimes taking Charles, who was also improving rapidly, with them. Kelly enjoyed these outings, but she much preferred it when they were alone.

They were quite literally alone in the house for a few days at the beginning of May when Charles Thorne went to a London clinic for some therapy treatment, and Mrs Banks and her husband decided to take the opportunity to have a holiday with their married daughter.

'Are you sure you'll be able to manage, dear?' Mrs Banks fussed.

'Yes, of course. You know I can cook,' Kelly said with a smile. By now she and the housekeeper were firm friends, especially as Kelly often ran errands like posting letters and doing odd bits of shopping for her. And she gave her some free time, too, because on fine days Kelly patiently walked beside Charles's wheelchair as he took a slow turn round the village. Slow, because nearly everyone he met stopped to chat with him, pleased to see him getting around more.

Byron decided to take Charles to London himself, and Kelly went with them so that she could see the capital. After settling Charles into the clinic, they booked into the same hotel, although their rooms were on separate floors. They spent nearly the whole of the next two days together as Byron took her all round the city. They went on an open-topped double-decker bus on a tour of all the sights, on a boat that took them along the River Thames from the Tower of London down to Greenwich Palace, round picture galleries and to Covent Garden where they watched the street entertainers before having dinner. And that was on the first day! The next they spent at nearby Eton College and Windsor Castle, then drove back to London to go over St Paul's Cathedral. Kelly thought that that wouldn't take very long, but Byron made her climb right to the top, to the cupola above the huge dome itself, where they could go outside and gaze at the panorama of the great city spread out before them. Then he rushed her back to the hotel to change before going on to the theatre to see the latest Lloyd Webber musical and for a late supper afterwards. Kelly enjoyed every exhausting minute of those two days, but when she finally dropped into bed that second evening she realised that she would be quite glad to get back to Ashdon Magna where she didn't have to share Byron with thousands of Londoners and other tourists. Although they'd been together the whole time, there hadn't been a minute when they'd actually been alone.

They left London immediately after breakfast, and Byron dropped Kelly off at Ashdon before driving on to his office. It felt strange, letting herself into an empty house. Kelly wandered round the house and garden with an almost proprietorial feeling, as if she belonged there and wasn't just a guest. The daffodils and narcissi had given way to tulips now; their rich silken heads making carpets of colour in the flower-beds. Kelly sat on the bench and looked around her, feeling happy and content. Or content for a moment at least, because she was filled, too, with eager anticipation at the thought of being alone here with Byron.

Since that one time he had never attempted to kiss her again, but Kelly knew instinctively that he was aware of her. And little things gave him away. Sometimes she would turn and catch him watching her, and he would arrange things so that they walked or sat together when they were with other people. He seemed to enjoy her company, even though she deliberately provoked him sometimes, even perhaps because she didn't let him take himself too seriously, and didn't appear to do so herself. Occasionally he became moody and withdrawn, but those times were much less frequent, and Kelly began to hope that he was well on the way to forgetting Elaine.

And that had become terribly important now, for with each passing day Kelly found herself falling for Byron more and more. Her heart jumped with happiness whenever she saw him, and tremors of awareness ran through her if they accidentally touched. She tried to conceal how she felt because she knew he would need time, but it was very hard. She dreamt about how it would feel to be held in his arms, and lived for the day when he would kiss her again. And what better time, she decided, than when they had the place all to themselves?

But on their first day back she was disappointed, because Byron rang to say that he was taking a client out to dinner and wouldn't be back till late. The second evening he brought a briefcase full of work home with him and disappeared into his study immediately after dinner, although he was appreciative of the meal she'd gone to a lot of trouble to prepare. Kelly began to feel exasperated, and wondered if he was deliberately trying to avoid her. So what did that mean—that he wasn't sure he could trust himself to keep a distance between them if he was alone with her? Kelly smiled at the thought and refused to think about the other side of the coin. Obstinately she watched the television until Byron emerged from his study at last.

'Hi,' she greeted him. 'Are you always this busy?'

'No, but the work piled up while I was away.' Kelly was sitting on the settee but he perched on the arm, looking down at her. 'Aren't you tired?'

She shook her head. 'I thought I'd walk down to the stables with you.'

'Hadn't you noticed? It's pouring with rain.'

'Well, I guess it won't kill me.' She got gracefully to her feet. 'And I could do with some fresh air.'

'Are you afraid to be alone here in the dark?'

'No, of course not. I've always felt completely safe.' She gave him a sharp look. 'Don't you want me to go with you, is that it?'

For answer he stood up and reached out to touch her hair lightly. 'We'll have to find you a mac.'

'There are lots in the cupboard,' Kelly remarked, her heart lightening.

But the atmosphere soon became tense again, because when she took a mac out and began to put it on, Byron said shortly, 'That was Elaine's.'

She stopped in the act of belting it. 'Does that mean you don't want me to wear it?'

'I'd rather you didn't, no.'

The anticipation of a moment ago in ruins, Kelly suddenly lost her temper and said. 'For heaven's sake, Byron, it's only an old mac. Not some sacred relic. Elaine's been gone for two years! What does it matter if I wear it or not?'

Byron's face had immediately tightened into a remote mask of withdrawal. 'Wear it, then,' he said shortly, and turned towards the door.

'No, it's OK. I'm sorry. I'll find something else.' She turned back to the cupboard but Byron didn't wait. He strode to the door and left it open for her to follow him. Kelly bit her lip and walked out to the porch where the rain splashed on to her face. Byron was already several yards away, striding along, bareheaded, and without bothering to look back to see if she was coming. Slowly Kelly went back inside and shut the door, knowing that everything was spoiled.

He must have stayed out a long time, because she was asleep when he got back, but she got up early to make him some breakfast.

'You don't need to do that,' he remonstrated when he came into the kitchen. 'I'm not entirely helpless.'

'No, I know.' She gave him an unhappy look. 'It was to sort of say sorry for last night.'

'Well, you shouldn't. I'm the one who ought to apologise. You were quite right,' he admitted ruefully. He saw her surprised look, but before she could say anything added quickly, 'Look, it's Saturday tomorrow. How about going out for the day? There's a town not too far away where they'll be celebrating May Day with all the traditional old festivities. I think you'd enjoy it.'

'It sounds great. I'd love to.'

'Good.' He smiled and sat down at the table in the sunny breakfast-room. 'Only thing is, I'll have to work late again tonight. So how about if I bring a take-away? Which do you prefer—Indian or Chinese?'

Kelly laughed as she sat down opposite him. 'Why don't you surprise me?'

He left soon afterwards and as Kelly cleared the dishes the thought came to her that this was what life would be like if she was married to Byron. And she found nothing wrong with the idea whatsoever.

The weather on that Saturday morning dawned bright and clear and promised to be warm and sunny. Kelly gave a sigh of relief; she had already planned what she was going to wear and didn't want to hide the outfit under a raincoat—even someone else's other than Elaine's. She had decided to wear one of the new-length layered denim skirts with a matching loose jacket and a thin sweater. Kelly had very good legs and she didn't see why she should hide them in trousers and sneakers when a skirt and high-heeled sandals looked so much better.

She ran downstairs eagerly and found that Byron had prepared breakfast for her today. 'Hey, you're doing me out of a job!'

'Don't get excited; it's only bacon and eggs.'

But to Kelly that morning anything would have tasted like nectar and ambrosia. Byron wouldn't even let her clear away and hurried her out to the car. It was quite a long drive through beautiful countryside, the trees bursting into leaf on this May morning, but Kelly found that she wasn't very interested in the countryside. Her eyes kept going to Byron, drinking in each feature, each tiny line, the slant of his dark brows, the line of his jaw, engraving them on her heart for ever.

They drew up eventually in a car park on the outskirts of a small town, and Byron said. 'There's a place near here where we can get coffee before we go on into the town.' They got out of the car, and as they began to walk along he said, 'You look very happy.'

'I am. Aren't you?'

'Yes,' he answered, as if it was a surprise to him to be happy. 'Yes, I am.'

'I feel all light and bubbly,' she told him. 'Like champagne.'

'And I offered you something as mundane as coffee.'

She smiled. 'Coffee will do—for the time being. But maybe I'll work on you to get a bottle of champagne before the day's out.'

That made him laugh, and he put his hand under

her elbow and walked her across to the coffee shop with its old bow window leaning out over the pavement.

'This place is really old,' Kelly commented as she looked up at the beamed ceiling, so low in places that Byron had to duck beneath them.

'The whole town is. It's an ancient market town, you see, and there's been some sort of community here since before the Roman invasion.'

Refusing to be overawed, Kelly said pertly, 'Oh, I see. This place is pretty new, then?'

But he didn't rise, merely looked amused and said, 'Mm, only fifteenth century.'

They drank their coffee and Byron glanced at his watch. 'There's a May Day procession through the streets this morning. If we go now, we should be in time to watch it.'

So they walked through to the oldest part of the town, mingling with people going the same way until they reached the market-place where the procession was due to pass. It was an ancient thoroughfare with lots of timber-framed buildings of Tudor origin mixed up with later stone Georgian houses and shops. The streets were cobbled and had decorative lamp-posts, each of them now garlanded with baskets of flowering plants. There were boxes of flowers too at many of the windows of the houses, and those that hadn't had hung out flags and buntings instead. It was a scene vibrant with life and colour, with the resurgence of hope that comes with the beginning of spring.

It was a little early for the procession, but there were several people in the market-square in what Kelly thought was just fancy dress, but Byron said were all traditional May Day costumes. One man, who was wearing an outfit completely covered in leaves, he told her was called the Green Man, and represented the

men who used to work in the forests. 'Look,' he
pointed. 'Do you see the name of that old pub over
there?'

Kelly looked and there he was, 'The Green Man',
pictured on the sign that hung outside the black and
white half-timbered inn, and wearing a costume not
unlike the man who was walking through the crowds,
collecting money for charity.

'Has the pub always had that name? How old do
you think it is?'

'Oh, yes, but the name goes back a lot further than
that; that building is probably only sixteenth century.
I'm pretty sure there was another inn of the same
name on the site in mediaeval times.'

Kelly gave him a wry look. 'There you go again.
Only sixteenth century! You make it sound like only
yesterday. You English just don't have any respect for
old buildings. If you lived in a country where there's
nothing much older than the eighteenth century, you
would look at them with the respect that's their due,'
she admonished him.

Byron tried to look contrite, but couldn't manage it.
'Sorry, but in Britain only BC is ancient; anything
after that is pretty commonplace.'

He was teasing her and she loved it, but pretended
to be angry with him. 'I'll have you know, if that
building could be shipped to Canada or the States, it
would have a million plus visitors a year.'

'Oh, I don't doubt it. But it wouldn't be the same,
would it? These old buildings are right here, they've
grown with the town. Canada is fine without them.
Look, there are some more people in costume. See
them? Come on, let's go nearer!'

Taking her hand, Byron led her to where a man was
wearing a most extraordinary costume of a 'horse'

suspended round his waist, so that it looked as if he was riding the horse, his legs hidden by the bright red silk panoply that hung from the horse's back. On his head the man wore a hat covered in flowers, and he carried a stick with a horse's head which he used to playfully tap the people he passed. 'What on earth is he supposed to be?' Kelly cried in astonishment, watching with delight as children gathered about the half-man, half-horse and then ran away, squealing with heady excitement as he ran at them with his stick.

'A hobby-horse,' Byron grinned. 'He's one of the Morris dancers.' He laughed at her expression. 'The Morris dancers are a group of men who wear traditional costume and perform very old dances, some as far back as the sixteenth century.'

'Men dancing together! This I've got to see. But haven't they got anything more with-it than the sixteenth century? The eighteenth or something?'

Byron laughed and smiled appreciatively. 'You know, you've got a very droll wit when you get going. Come on, let's walk up farther and meet the procession.'

Byron led her through the increasing throng until the street narrowed and they could go no further, the people all crowded round watching some men in the filthy black clothes of chimney sweeps, covered in soot and carrying bags of it over their shoulders. With them were teenage boys who carried ladders, and every time the sweeps saw a woman watching from an upper window they would put a ladder up to it, climb up and demand a kiss. They did pretty well for kisses on the ground, too, and there were many girls and women along the route who were trying to rub soot off their faces.

Instantly diverted, Kelly laughed with the rest until

one of the sweeps saw her and came over to claim his kiss. She gave a very feminine squeal and tried to dodge behind Byron, but the sweep threatened to empty his bag of soot over them, and Byron very unchivalrously stepped out of the way and left her to her fate.

'You heel!' Kelly said indignantly when she'd been well and truly kissed. 'How would you like it?' And she caught hold of Byron's jacket to try to rub some of the soot from her face on to his.

'Go on, love, give it to him,' a sweep called out, and several other people joined in. 'Kiss him. Go on. Don't let him get away with it.'

Standing on tiptoe, her eyes dancing with merriment, Kelly said, 'His majesty the King of the sweeps says I must.' And she leant forward to kiss him.

It was only a light peck as kisses go, but Byron drew his head back sharply, much to the derision of the crowd. 'Shame,' they called out. 'Put some soot over him, sweep.'

Kelly flushed and went to step away, but then Byron lifted his hands and gripped her shoulders. Kelly's eyes flew up to meet his, and what she saw there made her suddenly breathless. His eyes holding hers, a strange, taut look in his face, Byron bent to kiss her, his mouth finding hers in a few searing seconds that completely changed their relationship from that moment on.

It felt as if her heart had stopped beating, but Kelly instinctively knew that she must keep things light, and she somehow managed to laugh as she heard the crowd cheer. 'You coward! You were just afraid of being covered in soot.'

Byron blinked and gave a crooked grin. He took out his handkerchief to wipe the soot from their faces, his eyes grown troubled. 'Kelly,' he began, 'I don't . . .'

But she deliberately turned and pointed to the middle of the street. 'Oh, look, flower girls. Aren't they cute?'

She tried to keep her attention on the procession and not look at Byron, afraid of giving away her emotions, and she succeeded well enough, considering her heart was doing all kinds of crazy things. For with that one kiss Byron had brought to the fore the physical need she had so far managed to suppress. And was it the same for him? She sneaked a glance at him and he turned at the same time, almost as if they had the same thoughts. He wasn't smiling, his brows were drawn into a slight frown, but the awareness was there for him, too. There could be no mistake about that.

Too bemused to think coherently, Kelly somehow prattled on about the procession, watching the flower girls throwing out petals in front of the throng of young men and women who came dancing down the road, their music played for them by a band of pipers and fiddlers, the crowd on either side of the road clapping and joining in the song. Behind the long line of dancers were more people—dressed up, Byron told her when she asked, as Robin Hood and his men: Friar Tuck, Little John, Will Scarlett, and of course Maid Marion, managing to look demurely dressed but wanton too. Then there were more players with genuine Elizabethan instruments and men and women in Tudor dress who were supposed to be the ancient bailiff and burghers of the town.

After them came men dressed as Jack-o'-Lantern, Will-o'-the-Wisp and Hern the Hunter, all mystical creatures from the ancient past. And then the jingle of bells and merry music that heralded the Morris dancers that Byron had promised her. The men wore black breeches tucked into white socks and black shoes.

But over the socks they had tied pads covered in bells and ribbons that jingled whenever they danced. They had bells and ribbons, too, on the straps that crossed over their chests above their white shirts. And on their heads they had flower-covered hats like the man on the hobby-horse. The men carried sticks which they clacked against each other as they danced, but it was obviously hot work, because every time they came to a pub they demanded and got a pint of beer from the prettiest barmaid. After the Morris dancers, in pride of place, came the May Queen and her attendants, who held a flower-bedecked canopy over her head.

It was a long procession and by the end of it, when Byron had put his last coin into the last of the collecting boxes which had been rattled in front of them, Kelly had recovered her composure. Enough, anyway, to speak rationally and to hear above the thumping of her own heart.

They strolled back through the town, following in the wake of the procession, and whenever they passed a shop window Kelly secretly feasted her eyes on their reflections. Byron so tall and magnetically good-looking, and herself, beside him. Where she always wanted to be, she realised with heart-stopping certainty. Whatever came of this, she knew that she was head over heels in love.

Their steps tacitly slowed as they dawdled along. Most of the crowd had followed the procession down through the town to the park where maypole dancing was to take place later on. It left the streets strangely empty and quiet, with only scattered flowers petals to tell of its passing.

'Do you have anything like this in Canada?' Byron asked, his voice sounding strained.

'Not like this, no. But we do have the Calgary

Stampede.'

He laughed. 'Definitely not like this.' Reaching out, he took her hand. 'How about a drink or something to eat?'

'Can we go to that pub we passed, The Green Man?'

The pub was already quite crowded when they reached it, and they had to sit quite close to other people. Which was just as well really, Kelly decided; now wasn't the time to be alone and for private talk. Byron bought succulent home-made pork pies for them to eat and beer to drink, making Kelly remark that she'd have to jog a few more miles to get rid of the weight all this good food was making her put on.

'Nonsense.' Byron said definitely. 'You have a perfect figure.'

Kelly's eyes widened. 'I didn't think you noticed.'

He grinned. 'Oh, yes—I noticed.'

Kelly sat back in her seat, suddenly unable to eat. That grin had been frankly masculine and left her breathless. 'Tell me about those characters the men were dressed up as,' she managed faintly. 'What did you call them—Jack-o'-Lantern and Will-o'-the-Wisp?'

So Byron told her about the ancient legends and folklore, and they were still discussing it when they finished their snack lunch and began to walk through the town, making for the park where the afternoon's festivities were about to start. There was a craft market there, and for a while they wandered round the stalls. Kelly was intrigued by a straw figure called a corn-maiden and Byron immediately bought it for her, then made her blush by telling her that in the old days it was traditionally made with the last straw of the harvest as a fertility symbol.

The maypole dancing started, so they found a space on a piece of sloping ground where Byron spread his jacket on the grass and they sat on it to watch. There was tension between them now, an underlying awareness of each other that their outwardly calm appearance and idle talk couldn't dispel. It wasn't so much an emotional tenseness as one of excitement and anticipation. They sat with their shoulders touching, and presently Byron reached out to pick up her hand and began to idly play with her fingers. He didn't look at her very much, but, when they walked back to the car when the afternoon was over, he still held her hand in his. And as Byron drove slowly though the traffic back towards Ashdon Magna, they both knew that they had reached a turning point and that the road ahead was to bring them much closer.

They stopped for a meal on the way home. It was pleasant and she enjoyed it, but Kelly had the feeling that this was only a hiatus, and she longed to reach the Hall. But when they eventually got there she felt strangely shy and excused herself to go up and change. She didn't hurry, taking a shower and putting on a new dress with a halter neck that left her arms and shoulders bare but clung in all the right places.

When she went downstairs Byron was waiting for her in the drawing-room. He had lit the fire and stood in front of it, wearing casual trousers and a sweater without a shirt. Only the lamps near the fire were lit, so she had to walk further into the room before he could see her properly. He straightened up, his hand tightening on the glass he held, and stood gazing at her for a moment before he came forward to meet her.

'You look—very lovely,' he said slowly, an edge of desire roughening his voice. He lifted his hand as if to touch her, but then drew back. 'Would you like a drink?'

'Please. A gin and tonic.'

Byron poured it for her and as he gave it to her indicated the table that he'd set before the fire. 'I thought we might have a game of chess.'

'All right.' She sat down in one of the big wing chairs and Byron set out the board with its set of beautiful ivory figures. 'You can make the first move, if you like.'

His eyes came quickly up to hers and he gave a small smile, then moved his pawn to start the game.

It was warm in the room. The fire crackled and sent up flames that created dappled shadows across the bare skin of Kelly's arms. As the game progressed and she thought about her moves, she absently stroked her fingers along her arm in a gesture that was both sensual and provocative. She ran the tip of her tongue over lips gone dry and lifted her glass to drink, her eyes meeting Byron's as she did so. Desire was naked in his face for a moment, his features taut with inner tension. Kelly looked away, her heart racing, and was unable to concentrate so well on the game.

They didn't talk as they played: there was only the ticking of the old grandfather clock and the crackle of the fire to provide a background as they played out their battle on the board. A battle that had become far more than a game. Byron got up to put more logs on the fire and to refill their glasses. He stood over her for a moment, the glass in his hand, and Kelly raised wide, vulnerable eyes to meet his. She lifted her hand to take the glass, but Byron didn't release it straight away. He was looking down into her face, almost as if they had met again after a long time and he wanted to see how she'd changed. Because everything had changed now. After a long moment he blinked and sat down again, but as he did so their knees touched, sending a tingling shock-wave of desire coursing through her veins.

Kelly tried to go on playing, to concentrate on the game, but the moves they made were part of a bigger and far more enthralling game that they played out in the dimly lit room. The tension, the sense of anticipation, grew very strong. Kelly's eyes were wide with awareness and her lips parted in soft sensuality. The flame of desire in Byron's eyes darkened to hunger, and when she reached out to pick up one of the pieces he lifted his hand to catch hers. 'Checkmate, I think,' he said huskily, his voice unsteady.

Kelly dragged her eyes from his to look over the board. 'I lost!' she exclaimed on a breath of surprise.

'Yes.' Byron stood up and moved the table aside, then dropped his hands to gently caress her bare shoulders. She gasped, and Byron's grip tightened as he felt the quiver that ran through her. Slowly he lowered his head and found her mouth, the full softness of her lips against the hardness of his. Kelly gave a little moan of gladness, desire flooding through her like an erupting tide of red-hot lava. Byron's shoulders hunched and he drew her to her feet, her body brushing against his. His arms went round her and he held her close, his kiss deepening into hungry passion.

He began to stroke her back and her arms, his hands moving over her caressingly. His lips became possessive, demanding, and he took her mouth fiercely in an abandoned blaze of yearning. Kelly put her arms round his neck and clung to him, the world whirling in a dizzy vortex around her head, lost to everything but his closeness, the feel of him, the demanding passion of his kiss. Her mouth opened under his as she responded avidly, and she felt him give a low, gasping groan deep in his throat. He put his hands on either side of her face and kissed her until she felt faint and drowning. But then his mouth left hers as he kissed her neck, her eyes, the long column of her throat.

'Kelly. Oh, God Kelly!' He said her name with fierce urgency, his mouth returning with raging desire to her lips.

She moaned and drew back from him a little, half afraid of the intensity of her own feelings. They stared at each other, and she saw that his eyes were naked with hunger. Taking a deep breath, she reached out her hand to him. Byron took it and carried it to his lips in a gesture that was strangely tender, then turned off the lamps and pulled her down beside him to lie on the rug before the blazing fire.

CHAPTER SIX

IT WAS very late when Kelly woke the next morning. She had left the curtains open as usual and the sun was already high in the sky, sending beams that illuminated the dust motes dancing in the air. She smiled to herself happily as she remembered last night, and got quickly out of bed, eager not to waste a minute of the short time left to have the house to themselves. She showered, and as she dried herself noticed the faint marks on her skin where Byron had touched and held her in uncontrollable passion. Her eyes softened and she hurried to dress, longing to see him again, to read the reflection of her own feelings in his face.

He wasn't in the house, and when she looked in the garage she saw that the Land Rover, the vehicle he used when he visited the farms owned by the estate, was gone. A great surge of disappointment ran through her, but it was only a momentary feeling; Kelly was too happy for anything to really upset her. Perhaps Byron had an appointment to see one of the farmers. She would have liked to go with him, but he obviously hadn't wanted to take her. And it wasn't as if he'd ever taken her with him before when he visited the farms. But everything was different now, of course. Kelly wanted to be with him all the time, to share everything with him.

Going into the garden, she sat on one of the seats, her chin on her propped knees, a soft glow of contentment in her face. Life was so good. So very good.

Dreamily she began to think about the future: she would have to go back to Canada, of course, to sell off everything there. Maybe they could make that part of their honeymoon? Byron had never been to Canada, and it would be wonderful to take him touring round her own country and to introduce him to all her friends. She could just imagine their faces when she told them about the Hall and invited them to come over. A pang of sentimentality hit her at the thought of leaving Canada, but it was quickly gone when she compared it to living here with Byron. And anyway, they would be able to go back there for lots of holidays. Maybe she would keep the cabin in the mountains so that they could go back there for a month or so every year.

The time passed quickly as she sat in bemused euphoria, but presently she heard the sound of a car in the driveway and ran to meet it. It was Byron's Land Rover, but it was followed by two other cars. Kelly stopped precipitately and watched as several people got out and stood chatting in front of the house. Slowly she walked towards them.

Byron turned as she came up. He gave her a quick glance, but then began to introduce her to everyone. Kelly smiled politely and shook hands, but didn't get any of their names. It seemed that they had come to look at one of the mares which Byron wanted to sell, so Kelly went with them as they walked over to the stables. She hoped that Byron might make the opportunity to walk beside her for a moment, to say something about how he felt, or just to give her a special smile, but he strode along ahead of her with one of the farmers, deep in conversation about breeding stock.

The other people were nice enough to Kelly, asking

her questions and no doubt curious about her. But they all knew each other well, and once their curiosity was satisfied they resumed conversations that cut her out entirely. Mostly they talked about horses, and as she knew nothing about them they soon lost interest in her. The mare was saddled and ridden around the paddock, and paraded up and down as everyone made their own knowledgeable comments. Byron and the farmer struck the deal and then they all walked to the Hall where Byron invited them in for drinks.

After a couple of hours, Kelly began to think they would never go. But they all seemed quite at home, and Kelly realised that this Sunday gathering of neighbours was quite a regular thing. Mrs Banks had certainly prepared for it, because she found lots of packets of potato chips and other snacks in one of the store cupboards. Kelly emptied them into bowls and lingered longer than necessary in the kitchen in the hope that Byron might come out after her. But he didn't, and she had to carry the bowls into the drawing-room. Byron glanced towards her and she gave him an indignant look, but he didn't even smile, just took the glasses from the couple he was talking to and went to refill them.

It was almost two-thirty before the guests finally left. Kelly let Byron see them out and pushed open the french windows wide, finding the pall of smoke that hung in the room distasteful. She walked out onto the terrace and stood waiting with her back to the house, feeling suddenly nervous with tension. Her avid ears heard the shouts of goodbye and the cars pulling away, but it was several minutes afterwards before she heard Byron come into the drawing-room and step out on to the terrace. She waited breathlessly for him to come to her, to sweep her into his arms and kiss her. But nothing happened and Kelly slowly turned to see him just standing in the doorway, his hands thrust into his pockets. She ran to kiss him, but stopped short when he made no move towards her. Then she saw the cold, set look in his face.

'What is it? What's the matter?'

He threw her a brooding look and shook his head. 'It's nothing. I have some work to do in my study.'

He went to turn away, but Kelly ran forward and caught his arm. 'Wait a minute. Something must have happened. Why are you—like this? So—so cold?'

For a moment Byron hesitated, and she thought he wasn't going to explain, but then he said harshly, 'Last night happened.'

Despite herself, Kelly's eyes softened and she turned a glowing face up to his. 'Yes, I know. It was wonderful.'

'It was a mistake,' Byron interjected shortly. 'It should—it should have never have happened.'

She stared at him in consternation, unable for a moment to take it in. 'What—what do you mean?' she stammered, her heart beginning to shrink in dread.

'It was my fault,' he said with bitter self-reproach. 'I should never have let things go that far. I must have been mad. But you—you looked so love——' He broke off and turned away.

'I seem to remember that there were two of us involved,' Kelly said as steadily as she could, thinking she saw the reason for his inverted anger. 'It wasn't anyone's fault, for heaven's sake. I—I wanted it, too.'

His moody eyes swung back to her. 'It made a pleasant interlude, did it? Something to tell your friends when you go back to Canada, perhaps?'

Kelly's mouth fell open in astonishment as she stared at him. 'My God, is that what you think?'

Going closer, she tried to put her arms round him, but he held her off. 'Byron, I'm crazy about you. Don't you realise that? Last night was the most wonderful thing that ever happened to me. I—I'm in love with you.'

His brows flickered, and for a second she thought that she had reached him, but the cold mask came down again and he said grimly, 'You're too young to know what love means.'

'Of course I'm not. I . . .'

But he cut through her protests. 'Oh, you might think you're in love right at this minute. But really you're only in love with the idea of love. You think that what we—we did was romantic and wonderful, but one day soon you'll wake up and think of the boys back home, or of all that you want to do with your life.'

'I already know,' Kelly said fiercely. 'I want to spend the rest of my life here with you. I don't want to go back home.'

He smiled grimly at that. 'But you still call it home, don't you?' he pointed out with a kind of masochistic satisfaction. 'If you've any sense you'll just forget that last night happened—as I intend to do,' he said shortly.

She stared at him bleakly for a moment, and then shook her head, 'I can't do that. And neither can you. Not in a million years.'

'Well, it certainly won't happen again,' he told her with cruel emphasis.

Her face paled but Kelly said bravely, 'Maybe it won't. But I'm not going to let you forget, Byron. Every time you look at me you'll remember. And every time you touch me you'll want me again. Because last night you proved that you were crazy about mc, too, and I . . .'

'Crazy *for* you, perhaps,' Byron broke in roughly. 'But even crazier to have done anything about it.'

Kelly's head came up. 'Are you saying that you —you don't care about me, then?'

Byron's face closed into a frozen mask as he said, 'Yes,' very definitely. 'You turned me on—and that was all.'

Abruptly he turned to go in, but Kelly yelled after him, 'You're a coward, Byron. You get hurt and you're afraid to trust a woman again.' Slowly he turned to stare at her, his eyes murderous. Kelly quailed a little, but anger made her stand her ground. 'I'm me—Kelly Baxter,' she shouted at him. 'Not Elaine. I'm not the one who jilted and hurt you. I've told you I love you, and I mean it. And I'm not going to leave you. No matter how rude and nasty you are to me, you're not going to drive me away. Even if Cousin Charles tells me I've got to leave, I'll still stay in the village and I'll make darn sure you know I'm there. Because I love you, Byron, whether you like it or not,' she said passionately. 'So you'd better just darn well get used to the idea. OK?'

But he didn't answer, just gave her a fiercely angry look, turned on his heel and went inside.

Kelly moved forward as if to follow him, and then stopped. She had said everything that mattered, everything she could say. All that remained to be seen was whether it was the right thing, but the way Byron had stormed off, she began to have terrible doubts. Maybe she should have been soft and coaxing instead of going off like that? But he had made her so angry, and it was in her nature to go all out for what she wanted.

The rest of the afternoon dragged interminably. Byron stayed in his study with the door firmly shut, while Kelly sat around and mourned for the lost hours they were wasting. Because tonight Jim and Enid Banks were due back, and tomorrow morning Jim was going to London to collect Cousin Charles. The house would be full again and there would be no more chances for making love in front of the fire—or anywhere else, probably—even if she could persuade Byron to give up this crazy attitude. She cooked dinner, and at six-thirty went to the study and walked in.

She caught Byron gazing moodily through the window instead of concentrating on the documents spread out on the desk in front of him. 'Hi,' she said breezily. 'Dinner in half an hour. Would you like a drink first?'

'Would it be too much trouble to knock?' he answered acidly.

'Yes, it would. I'm not a servant. And I'm definitely not just a guest any more,' Kelly added deliberately.

Byron got to his feet, his face stiffening. 'I suppose you think you have the right to say that, but . . .'

'Yes, I do.' Moving closer, Kelly looked steadily up at him. She smiled softly. 'Is it so very bad?'

His eyes went over her, taking in her slim figure, remembering how she had looked when the curves of her naked body had cast such seductive shadows in the firelight. Byron's jaw tightened and a pulse beat in his throat. Kelly's breath caught in her chest as she saw the dark desire in his eyes. Her lips parted sensuously and she stepped closer and put up a hand to touch him. But Byron quickly reached up and caught her wrist. 'You little witch,' he said hoarsely.

'A witch?' Kelly gave an indignant laugh and shook her head. 'No. You can't blame me for how you feel, Byron. I didn't *make* you fall for me. At first I didn't even like you. And I didn't exactly ask to fall in love with you, either. But I'm willing to give up my home, my country, everything that I know and love, to be with you.'

Still holding her wrist, Byron reached up to gently touch her face, a line at his mouth deepening with bitter irony. 'You're very brave, Kelly. Full of courage. I don't . . .' He broke off and, letting her go, turned away. 'It wouldn't work,' he said shortly. 'There are too many differences between us, just as there were w——'

'With Elaine,' Kelly supplied when he broke off. 'Go ahead, say it. Saying her name can't hurt me.' She sighed and said under her breath. 'Heaven knows, she's alive enough in this house.'

'All right, with Elaine.' Byron swung round to face her, and said earnestly. 'Can't you see? You're still only twenty-one. I'm ten years older than you. You've lived all your life in a big city.' He held up a hand as she began to speak. 'I know what you're going to say: that you love it here. But that's only because it's so new for you, and because you love the history of it all. But even the most beautiful scenery can pall when you see it day after day, especially in the winter. And you'll soon get tired of a small community like this. You were even bored at lunch time when those neighbours were here, I could tell.'

'I wasn't bored,' Kelly protested. 'I just didn't know them well enough. But I admit I wanted them to leave.' Her eyes met his. 'I wanted to be alone with you again,' she said huskily.

Byron's teeth clenched as he tried to withstand the compelling sensuousness in her wide grey eyes. Eyes that he had so willingly drowned in last night. 'It wouldn't work,' he said, even more harshly than he'd intended.

'But we could try. After all, we do have that—that basic chemistry going for us and . . .'

'You mean sexual attraction,' Byron cut in bluntly.

'Yes, I suppose I do. But it's more than that, isn't it?'

'Is it?' His voice was heavy, doubting.

'I know it is for me,' she replied sincerely.

Byron looked intently into her face for a few moments, then gave a short laugh and shook his head. 'You young girls, you're always so certain of your own feelings—to start with.' His voice became bitter. 'It's only when the euphoric glow starts to fade that you suddenly face reality and realise you've committed yourself for the rest of your life.'

'It won't be like that,' Kelly protested. 'I'm sure of my feelings for you.'

'How *can* you be sure?' Byron argued angrily. 'We've only known each other such a short time.'

'Long enough to know how much we needed each other last night,' she reminded him earnestly.

For a moment Byron's face softened, but then he said, 'That was physical attraction, nothing more.' He looked at her mutinous face and added shortly. 'It has to be that way, Kelly. Don't you understand? Elaine and I had known each other for years. She thought she was sure of her feelings too, and if she didn't know after all that time, how can you possibly be sure after only a matter of weeks?'

'Maybe that was the trouble with her,' Kelly pointed out quickly, not liking the dismissive note in his voice. 'Maybe you just knew each other too well. Charles wanted her to marry you, didn't he, to keep the estate? Perhaps she felt that she was being coerced into it.'

'Nonsense,' Byron said sharply. 'There was no

coercion, she was always free to choose. In fact, she was encouraged to meet other people, other boys her own age, but she never wanted to. That's why I went ahead. There seemed to be no point in waiting.'

A brooding look came into his face and Kelly stepped quickly forward and put her arms round his waist. 'But now Elaine's gone,' she said softly. 'She realised she'd made a mistake and put it right before too much harm was done. It would have been much worse if she'd gone through with the marriage first. Can't you forget about her?' she pleaded. 'All that's in the past. She's gone—and I'm here. And I *know* how I feel. Otherwise last night would never have happened.' And, slipping her arms around his neck, Kelly lifted her head to kiss him.

Immediately Byron put his hands on her arms as if to push her away, but she was kissing him softly, exploringly, her lips caressing his, the sweet taste of them evoking such tantalising memories that he groaned and pulled her roughly to him. He kissed her hard on the mouth, the compelling demand in it betraying his deep need of her.

But when he lifted his head the frown was still there in his eyes. Taking her hand, Byron said forcefully, 'Kelly, I want you to promise me something. I want you to try to be objective.' He saw the look in her eyes and smiled wryly. 'Oh, I know you think that's impossible, but you've told me you're an adult, so I want you to think like one. OK? And I want you to think of yourself. To remember the life you had in Canada and compare it with here. So do it sensibly, realistically. Think about what you'd be giving up if you stayed on here with Charles and I. Will you promise to do that?'

'Yes, all right.' She stepped back and smiled. 'And

now I think we'd better go and eat.' Having made the promise, Kelly would keep it, but she thought that being objective was going to be very difficult. Who could be—or wanted to be—realistic when they were in love, for heaven's sake?

Instead of using the big dining-room, Kelly had set places for them in the much smaller breakfast-room where she had drawn the curtains and lit candles in a silver holder. Kelly had hoped that the romantic setting would seduce Byron into a softer mood, but he stubbornly resisted her efforts, moving his chair further away and switching on the over-head light. Kelly didn't push it; she supposed it had been rather an obvious ploy, but she at least got him to tell her of his boyhood and eventually he relaxed and it was a pleasant meal. Only if their hands happened to touch or their eyes caught did the tension momentarily return, but you couldn't continually live on such a knife-edge, and Kelly quickly dispelled it by making some light remark.

Towards the end of their meal they heard a car draw up outside and the sound of familiar voices and knew that Jim and Enid Banks were back. Kelly's eyes clouded wistfully, wondering if they would ever have an opportunity to be so completely alone again. And whether she could work on Byron enough for it to be any good if they did. Byron must have realised her thoughts because he put a finger under her chin and said, 'Remember you made me a promise, Kelly. I expect you to keep it.'

'Yes, all right.' She stood up and began to collect the dishes on to a tray. 'I'd better go and say hello to Mrs Banks.'

But obviously she hadn't sounded convincing enough, because Byron got quickly to his feet and caught her arm. 'I mean it, Kelly. You've got to put all the—the physical attractions aside and concentrate on deciding whether you really want this kind of life.'

Kelly looked at him, and then lifted her hands up to her face with a wild kind of laugh. 'Forget the physical side? Do you know what you're saying? What you're asking? Could *you* do it? Oh, Byron, all I want is to be close to you. Is that too much to ask?' He was silent, his face taut. With a sob Kelly covered her eyes, her face cupped in her hands, her fingers pressing hard into her skin.

'Kelly, don't. Please don't cry.'

Byron went to pull her hands away, but she swung away from him. 'Damn you, I'm not crying. You just made me so darn angry. Why won't you trust me? I trusted *you*!'

His jaw clenched, 'I didn't intend that to happen,' he said tightly. 'Things just got out of hand.'

'But I'm *glad* they did.' Going up to him, Kelly put her arms round his waist, under his jacket. 'Aren't you? Aren't you glad?'

He looked down at her for a long moment, then put his hand in her hair and kissed her lightly. 'Yes,' he admitted. 'It was perfect, wonderful.' He sighed and laid his head against her hair. 'You make me feel like Samson,' he murmured. 'I try to be so strong, but I only have to look at you and all my resolve melts away. I *ache* for you, Kelly. An ache so bad it's almost like a physical pain deep inside me.'

'Well, if you feel like that . . .' She raised hopeful eyes to his.

But Byron shook his head. 'Pains can be cured, or they go away. I can't trust how you say you feel.

I'm sorry, Kelly, but there it is. Once bitten and all that. If you were older, perhaps. Who knows. But . . .'

'So just how old do I have to be before you believe me?' Kelly broke in in helpless anger. 'Thirty? Or forty, perhaps? Tell me, Byron, if I go on telling you how much I care about you until I'm forty, will you believe me then?'

He started to protest but she flung away from him, picked up the tray and strode to the door. But she had to stop to try to open it and one of the glasses slid off the tray and fell to the floor. 'Oh, hell!'

'Easy.' Byron picked it up and put it back on the tray. 'It's all right, it didn't break.' He held her arm for a moment and was about to say something, but saw that she was biting her lip hard to keep back tears, so he merely opened the door and let her go through.

Mrs Banks was already in the kitchen, eager to tell of her holiday with her daughter and grandchild, so Kelly had ample time to recover. She stayed in there for over half an hour, and then chose a book from one of the shelves in Charles's study. A novel, something that she could lose herself in. Byron was in the drawing-room, seated in an armchair and with the television set on. Kelly stood in the doorway and said, 'I'm going up to bed. Goodnight.'

'Are you tired?'

'No. I'm going to read.' And she indicated the book.

'I'll turn the television off if you'd rather read in here.'

'No.' She shook her head. 'Goodnight.'

'Goodnight, Kelly.'

He didn't get up, and she somehow resisted the

temptation to go to him, instead turning quickly
away and running upstairs. But when she got into
bed the book didn't hold her after all, and it was a
long time before she at last put out the light and fell
asleep.

The following morning Kelly spent with Mrs Banks,
making sure that everything was perfect for
Charles's homecoming. He arrived about lunch
time, looking drawn, but seemed pleased by the fuss
they made of him although, being male, he
pretended not to be.

'All these flowers. And a fire in my room. It really
isn't necessary, you know.' But he settled back in his
armchair with a sigh of relief and smiled at her.
'What have you been doing while I've been away?'

Pulling up a stool, Kelly sat down at his feet and
began to tell him all about their trip to see the May
Day festivities, her face animated as she described
the procession, so that Charles laughed in amusement. 'I'm glad Byron took you there; I told him to
look after you.'

'Yes, he—he took care of me,' Kelly agreed,
trying to hide the wistfulness in her eyes.

Byron had gone to his office that day, and she only
saw him at dinner, when Charles was with them, of
course. And afterwards the two men spent some
time going over estate affairs, because even though
Charles could take no active interest he still liked to
know every detail of what was going on, to be master
of his own, albeit very mortgaged, property, even if
not master of his own body.

When their discussion was over, Charles said that
he was tired, and went to his room where Jim Banks
would help him to bed, but Byron stayed in his

study. Kelly got the distinct impression that he was avoiding her, an impression that was borne out when she saw a great deal less of him than she normally did in the following couple of weeks. His evenings seemed to be full of meetings, and the days he spent on estate work took him out all the time. Kelly didn't like it, but she recognised that maybe he needed some space for a while—enough to miss her, anyway. She spent the time pleasantly enough with Cousin Charles who was teaching her all about the local history in return for more chess lessons. And when she had time alone Kelly kept her promise to Byron by trying to be objective and analyse her feelings. Both of which were virtually impossible. To ask her to define her feelings was to ask her to define love. And who could ever break down that exhilarating excitement, that need to be with one person and that person only? How to define a feeling so strong that it took possession of you and held you subject to it for the rest of your life? Kelly couldn't, but she'd promised so she tried to be practical and think of what she'd had in her old life. But the very fact that she now thought of it as her old life spoke for itself. And she had no wish to go back to that life, especially now that her parents were dead.

That thought brought her up short for a moment, and made her wonder if she was just trying to find a relationship to replace the one that she'd lost, but if that was the case why hadn't she turned to someone in Canada? There had been men enough who'd wanted to date her, but she'd turned away from them. Kelly thought as long and as hard as she could, and in the end was glad that she'd done so, because now there was reason to add to what instinct had always told her. She was in love with Byron and

wanted to spend her life with him. Now all she had
to do was to convince him of that.

The weekend came round again and Byron could
find no excuse to go out. And anyway, Daisy
Pickman had gone away for a couple of weeks, so he
had to take care of the horses. Kelly saw him go out
early on the Saturday morning and followed him
down to the stables.

'Hi. Want a hand?'

'No, it's OK, thanks. I can manage.'

'OK.' But she didn't go away, just leaned against
the wall and watched him as he groomed one of the
horses.

'Aren't you going out with Charles today?' Byron
asked with studied casualness.

'No. I thought I'd spend the day with you.'

'And what if I don't want you with me?' he
demanded impatiently.

'Don't you?'

The question was husky, provocative, and he
turned quickly to look at her. It was a hot day and
she was wearing only a thin shirt above her jeans,
the material taut across her breasts. Byron licked lips
suddenly gone dry. 'Kelly, you promised to think
things through.'

'And I've kept my promise.' She smiled with
some irony. 'I've had plenty of time to think this last
couple of weeks.'

'And the result?' He dropped the curry-comb and
came over to her, his hands thrust into his pockets.

Straightening, Kelly said earnestly, 'I really
looked at it from every angle. I even wondered if I
was on the rebound in some crazy kind of way
because of my parents. I *really* thought about it, I
want you to know that.'

'But you still feel the same,' he said shortly.

'*And* I still feel the same. But while I was doing all that thinking, it made me wonder about you; why you feel the way you do about me.'

His eyebrows went up. 'What do you mean?'

'Well, you do care about me, don't you? And if you say it's just sex, Byron, I shall hit you, because I know it's more than that.'

He gave a short laugh. 'It seems you've answered your own question, then.'

'But I want to hear you say it,' she insisted.

His brows flickered, but then he nodded. 'Yes, I care about you.'

'Well,' Kelly gave an inner sigh of relief. 'That's something, at any rate. Now all I have to ask is why.'

'Why? Because—because you're beautiful, and vital. Because you turn me on, and because I miss you like hell when we're apart.' He paused and gave a crooked smile. 'Is that enough?'

'No.' She was inwardly aglow with pleasure, but gave a definite shake of her head. 'It isn't. Because I want to know if it's really *me* you care for—or is it because I remind you of Elaine?'

Immediately a stunned look came into his eyes, a look so full of surprise and incredulity that Kelly's question was instantly answered. Not that she'd ever needed to ask it; she had been quite sure in her own mind that *she* was in his thoughts, but Kelly had decided that it wouldn't hurt Byron to have to look at his own feelings.

'No!' he said at once. 'Good God, you surely don't think that?' Reaching out, he took hold of her arms and looked at her earnestly. 'Apart from that very first time, you have never reminded me of

Elaine. Not physically, anyway, although I admit that sometimes you make me think of her. I remembered her once when you had an armful of flowers because she used to go out and pick them for the house. And sometimes you made me realise what I had missed by not being married.'

'But you've let her come between us,' Kelly said gently.

'No, not her. Just the bitterness she left behind.'

'I might take some convincing of that.'

There was something in her voice that brought his eyes up swiftly to meet hers. Then he grinned. 'Might you, indeed.'

'Mm. But I'm willing to take something on account.'

Byron laughed and there was a note of happiness in it. 'You'd better come here, then,' he invited huskily.

Moving to lean against him, Kelly put her arms round his neck. 'Do you believe me now?' she asked, lifting a hand to stroke it along his jaw-line.

He nodded slowly, still not entirely convinced. 'Yes, but I still think you ought to take more time.'

But Kelly shook her head. 'No, it isn't me, it's you.'

'Perhaps you're right.' Bending his head, Byron lightly kissed the edge of her eyebrow. 'Your skin is so soft,' he murmured, moving on down her cheek to her throat.

Kelly's eyes closed in pleasure and she moved against him as she felt his body harden. 'Do you *really* want more time?' she asked on a breathless note.

'I want *you*, *I need you*. Dear God, I do.' He took her mouth hungrily. 'I've been going mad these last two weeks, having you so near, remembering the night we were together, how wonderful it was.' He held her close, kissing her as he spoke, his hand low on her waist, pressing her against him so that she gave a low moan of frustration.

'Oh, I know. I know. It isn't so bad during the day when you're not here. Then I only miss you. But at night, when I hear you go by my room . . . Oh Byron, I don't want you to go by.'

'My little love.' He kissed her so fiercely that he hurt a little, but Kelly held him just as tightly, her fingers digging into his shoulders. But suddenly he broke away and stepped back, a film of sweat on his brow. He held her at arm's length, his breathing ragged. 'If I come to you tonight,' he said unevenly, 'someone might find out.'

'Is that so very terrible? Does it matter?'

'It wouldn't to me.' He gave her a direct look. 'But it might to Charles.'

Kelly frowned. 'But he sleeps downstairs, he . . .' She broke off. 'Oh, I see.'

'Quite. He might not like the idea of me making love to a guest under his own roof. Especially . . .'

'Especially as you were once engaged to his daughter,' Kelly finished for him. 'Oh, hell, why is nothing ever simple?' She bit her lip, thinking hard, then turned a bright face up to his. 'But why shouldn't it be simple? Why don't we just tell him?'

'Tell him we're lovers?' Byron exclaimed in a startled voice.

'Tell him that we're *in* love,' she corrected. 'And if he doesn't like it—well, I'll move out and stay in the village at the Horn of Plenty again.'

'But if we tell him that, he'll expect us to get

married,' Byron pointed out. 'He has old-fashioned standards, does Charles.'

'And so have I,' Kelly stated definitely. 'And I expect it too.'

Byron began to laugh a little, but stopped when he saw the seriousness in her face. 'God, Kelly, you're so sure, you frighten me sometimes. Surely marriage can wait until . . .'

'No,' Kelly broke in. 'I'm not going to sell myself short just because some other girl let you down. This is love, Byron, not some kind of a test.' Her face flushed angrily. 'If you want me, then you're going to have to marry me. I'm not going to hang around on—on sufferance until you finally convince yourself that you can trust me. So you'd better just make up your mind what it is you want.'

She glared at his bemused expression, then turned on her heel and began to stride away, but Byron reached out and caught her wrist. 'I've made up my mind.'

'What?' She had to turn back because he held her, but Kelly was still so annoyed that she hardly heard him.

'I said that I have given the matter a great deal of careful consideration and I have made up my mind.'

'You—you have?' She was staring at him now.

'Yes. I love you very much, Miss Baxter, and I would like to marry you as soon as possible.'

Her eyes grew misty. 'Well, you—you certainly took your time.'

'Mm.' He waited and, when she didn't speak, said impatiently, 'Well, aren't you going to say anything?'

'Don't rush me. A girl has to think about these

things!' But as he burst into laughter she threw herself into his arms. 'Oh, yes, yes, my darling. Oh, Byron, I'm so crazy about you.'

He hugged her tightly and they kissed in exuberant happiness. 'When shall we tell Charles?' he asked when he at last released her. 'Tonight?'

'No, not tonight.' She looked lovingly into his eyes. 'Why don't we wait until tomorrow?'

He smiled, his eyes already alight with anticipation. 'And I'll come to you tonight.'

'Yes,' she breathed, lifting her mouth to be kissed. 'Tonight.'

When Byron let her go, Kelly's cheeks were again flushed, but not with anger this time. He smiled at her and said with mock authority, 'Now, woman, will you let me finish grooming this poor horse? I've got to exercise him yet, and the foal wants taking out to the paddock to join his mother.'

'I could take him for you,' Kelly offered, 'I've done it before with Daisy.'

'All right. I'll put a halter on him in a minute.' He finished grooming the stallion, saddled him and tied him up outside, then put a halter over the foal's head. 'Sure you can manage him?'

'Of course. He's a sweetie.'

'Right. I'll go for a gallop over the fields, then. Be back in about an hour. He grinned at her with a ruefully appealing look. 'An hour can be a very long time, you know.'

Kelly laughed and let him kiss her, responding eagerly to the new possessiveness of his lips. 'Oh, Byron,' she murmured, 'everything is going to be so wonderful from now on.'

'I know. I feel that, too.' He let her go and swung himself easily up on to the stallion's tall back. 'See you later.'

He trotted out of the stableyard, turning to wave
as he reached the edge of the woods. Kelly watched
him go and then turned in the other direction,
leading the foal towards the paddock. The sun shone
in her face and she lifted her head to it. It was a
perfect spring day, the May blossom already
drowning the bushes along the hedgerow. The scent
of it was strong in the still air and in Kelly's happy
imagination the thick fall of blossom resembled a
long bridal veil. She laughed happily to herself and
decided that after she had put the foal in the paddock
she would go for a walk up into the meadows in the
hills that overlooked the house, find somewhere
quite alone, and lie down in the sun to daydream
about the future.

The track turned with the hedge and she strolled
along, the foal, smelling warm and pleasantly
horsey, ambling along at her side. Kelly thought she
saw someone leaning on the paddock wall, near the
gate, and blinked, her eyes still squinting against the
sun. She was right, there was someone there. A girl.
Shorter than herself and with trendy, close-cropped
dark hair.

'Hi,' Kelly greeted her, thinking she must be
someone from the village, someone Daisy knew,
perhaps.

The girl turned to look at her fully, her eyes
running over Kelly speculatively, studying her
almost. And there was something in her eyes that
made Kelly come to a sudden stop and stare at her.
Glancing down, she saw a suitcase at the girl's feet,
but hardly needed it to confirm her instinctive guess.
'You're Elaine,' she said on a slow, reluctant
breath.

The girl nodded. 'Yes, that's right. I've come home.'

CHAPTER SEVEN

KELLY stared at the other girl, too shattered to speak for several minutes. But then the foal pushed against her impatiently, eager to rejoin his mother. 'I—I'll just put the foal in the field,' Kelly said unsteadily.

She opened the gate and took him in, and was about to turn him loose when Elaine said. 'Hadn't you better take the halter off first?'

'What? Oh, sure. Of course.' The foal wanted to get to his mother, he kept backing away and she had difficulty in taking his halter off, and it didn't help of course to know that Elaine, the expert on horses, was watching.

The foal was free at last and cantered away. Kelly came out on to the track and said rather helplessly. 'My name's Kelly Baxter. I'm a kind of cousin of yours, and I'm staying up at the Hall.'

'Yes, I know.' Elaine spoke evenly, her voice giving nothing away. But then, neither did her eyes or face. 'You're from Canada.'

'That's right.' Kelly answered in surprise. 'How did you know.'

'I still have friends in the village,' Elaine replied unemotionally.

She didn't say anything else, the silence becoming tense and heavy, to Kelly, anyway—Elaine didn't seem to notice it at all. To break it, Kelly said, 'I guess you want to see Cousin Charles. Shall I—would you like me to tell him that you're here?'

'No.' The other girl shook her head. 'It's you I wanted to see.'

'Me?' Kelly gave her a startled look. 'Why should you want to see me?'

'I heard about you. I was told that you were trying to take my place—and succeeding,' she added on a soft note that seemed suddenly full of menace.

Kelly looked at her warily for a moment, but then felt a flash of anger when she remembered Charles's hurt and Byron's bitterness. 'What the hell did you expect when you walked out on people who loved you?' she flashed. 'Did you expect them to sit around moping, just waiting for you to decide to come back? So Cousin Charles is starting to enjoy life a little more. My God, doesn't he deserve it after all he's been through?'

Elaine's eyes widened a little at her tirade. 'So you blame me, do you?'

Biting her lip, Kelly shook her head. 'No. No, I don't blame you. I guess every girl makes some kind of a mistake when they're young. It was just running off the way you did, without having the courage to face up to your mistake.' She shook her head again. 'I know I shouldn't judge you, but you left such a lot of—of unhappiness behind you. Surely if you felt you had to go away, you could have put things right first?'

For a long moment Elaine didn't speak, then turned and leaned against the wall again. 'The circumstances were extremely difficult. My father—but you know my father,' she said with a mirthless laugh.

'No. Not the man that you know. I think you'll find that he's changed a lot. Cripples can't afford to be stern martinets, they're too dependent on others. Disability teaches humility.'

Elaine turned her head to stare at her. 'When I went to see him at the hospital, he refused to see me.'

'Yes, I know. Maybe it was too soon.'

'No.' Elaine shook her head. 'I went three times.' She paused. 'But if he's changed, as you say . . . Do you think there's any chance that he will see me now?'

The question was asked very directly, and with it was a tacit admission that Elaine no longer suspected Kelly of deliberately trying to usurp her. The latter shook her head. 'I don't know for certain. He—he never talks about you, you know. And everything to do with you, he's had put away. I'm sorry,' she added uncomfortably.

'It's all right. I knew that already.'

Kelly gave her a quick glance of speculation; if she knew that then she must also know that Byron had taken her portrait to her bedroom and had the room cleaned regularly, ready for if she ever came back. For the first time, a shiver of fear for her own happiness ran down Kelly's spine. But she said, 'But what have you got to lose by asking to see him? I'm sure he misses you terribly. Although he tries very hard not to show it, of course. Why don't you try?'

Elaine smiled a little, and Kelly wondered if *she* had changed very much since she'd been away. She was dressed conservatively enough, in a navy blue skirt and short-sleeved blouse, a cardigan hanging from her shoulders. Her face was eye-catching rather than pretty, her features clear-cut and defined, but there was more than a hint of hardness about her mouth and in that steady self-composure.

'Perhaps I might. Is Byron at home?'

That question, too, was asked unemotionally, but it made Kelly quake inwardly as she wondered how Byron would react when he came face to face with his ex-fiancée. 'Yes, he's home. That is, he isn't at the moment, he's out riding, but he probably won't be all that long.'

The other girl nodded. 'You say my father never speaks of me; does he talk about me with Byron?'

'Not that I know of. I don't think so. But then, I've only been here a couple of months.'

'Not very long,' Elaine agreed. 'But perhaps long enough.'

She didn't elucidate and Kelly didn't ask her. After a moment Kelly said diffidently, 'Would you like to come up to the house and have a coffee or something? Have you come very far?'

Elaine gave her a faintly amused glance that suddenly reminded Kelly vividly of Cousin Charles. 'Quite the hostess,' she commented.

Kelly stiffened. 'I'm sorry.'

'Oh, don't be. I know the circumstances are unusual, to say the least. No, I won't come up to the house yet. I think I'll wait until Byron gets back to talk to him first. How long did you say he'd be?'

'About an hour. He's exercising one of the horses.' Kelly paused, then said deliberately, 'Aren't you rather taking it for granted that Byron will want to see you? After all, walking out on him when you did was rather worse than just leaving home, wasn't it?'

Despite herself, a note of antagonism had crept into Kelly's voice, and Elaine looked at her sharply. 'So you're on Byron's side, are you?' Then she shrugged. 'It was two years ago; if Byron was annoyed, he will have got over it by now, surely?'

'Annoyed?' Kelly exclaimed. 'That's—that's rather understating it, isn't it?' Realising that she was giving her feelings away, she drew herself up and said. 'I'm sorry, you have every right to tell me that it's none of my business, but I—well, I *like* Cousin Charles and Byron. They've both been very kind to me. You see, I—I don't have anyone of my own now.'

'Yes, I heard that too.' But there was no visible softening in Elaine's face. It was almost as if she had no feelings. But then Kelly's intuition came to the fore and she realised that the other girl was so afraid of being rebuffed again that she was deliberately keeping all her feelings in check.

Kelly's face softened and she said, 'Why don't you come to the stables and wait for Byron there? You can sit down then. And I'll make a mug of coffee, if you like.'

'All right, thanks.'

Elaine picked up her case and fell into step beside Kelly as they walked back along the track. Kelly wondered what the other girl would think if she knew that Byron and she had got engaged only that morning. But more than anything she worried about how Byron would feel when he saw Elaine waiting for him. Would he be angry? Would he turn on his heel and ignore her? Or would he again realise all that he had missed by not marrying her?

When they reached the stables, Elaine sat down on the bench outside while Kelly went into the tackroom and used Daisy Pickman's kettle to make a mug of coffee. She took it outside and saw that Elaine had closed her eyes. Like that, she suddenly looked very young, very vulnerable, and very tired. But she quickly opened them when she heard Kelly, and took the mug with a word of thanks.

'Look,' Kelly said awkwardly, 'I know you think Byron will be over you—and I'm sure he is,' she added hastily. 'But I think it would be better if I warned—if I let him know you're here first. Don't you agree?'

'If you like.' Elaine said it indifferently, almost as if she didn't care about Byron, and Kelly felt another surge of anger.

'Right,' she said shortly. 'I guess I'll go walk down to meet him, then.'

She waited, but Elaine merely nodded and bent to drink her coffee, so Kelly turned and walked towards the woods, her steps gradually hurrying until she broke into a run, wanting to put as much time and space as possible between Elaine and Byron before she told him. But when she reached the edge of the wood there was no sign of him, so she had to stay there and wait, afraid to climb the hills in search of him in case he came from a different direction and she missed him.

He came into view about a quarter of an hour later, cantering easily over the brow of a hill over to the west. Kelly jumped up from the tree trunk she'd been using as a seat and ran to meet him. He laughed when he came up to her and reached down to take her hand. 'Don't tell me you're missing me already. I . . .' He broke off as he saw her face. 'What is it? What's happened?' he demanded urgently.

'Oh, Byron.' She looked up at him in distress. 'I don't know how to tell you. You've got to prepare yourself for a shock. I . . .'

'Is it Charles? Is he . . .?' His hands tightened on the reins as he prepared to gallop back to the house.

'No! No, it's not Charles. Oh, Byron—it's Elaine. She's—she's here.'

He stared at her, a stupefied look in his eyes. 'Here? At the house? Has Charles seen her?'

'No. That is, she hasn't been up to the house yet. She wants to see you first. She's waiting for you at the stables.'

'*Is she?*' Byron's head lifted, and he looked grimly in the direction of the stables, almost as if he could see through the thick depths of the trees. His face had gone very hard and pale, the bitter lines suddenly back around his mouth. It was a look that tore at Kelly's heart, and she cursed Elaine for not leaving them in peace.

He began to trot forward but Kelly called out 'Byron' with a note of desperation in her voice, and he immediately reined in and looked back at her. Slowly she went up to him and said urgently, 'Please. Will you remember something when you see her? Will you remember that I love you *very much*?'

His face softening, Byron dismounted and put his arm around her waist. He held her for a long moment, and Kelly felt his lips touch her hair, and when he loosened his hold he said. 'Why don't we walk back together?'

She hugged him and said, 'Fine. But—but I shall quite understand if you want to go on ahead and see her alone.'

'No. I've waited two years, I think I can wait a while longer.'

Kelly was still so uncertain of what his reaction was going to be that she wasn't sure whether she liked that last remark or not. They began to walk back, Byron setting an unhurried pace, and with his arm still around her waist, but he was silent all the way and when the stables came into sight she could feel the way his body tautened as tension increased with every stride. Kelly remembered how he'd lost control of his emotions when he'd mistaken *her* for Elaine, and could but dread the outcome of this meeting.

Elaine was still sitting on the bench, but she got to her feet as they turned into the yard. Kelly tried to watch both of them at the same time to see how they would react, but they were prepared and their expressions, Elaine's especially, gave nothing away. Byron just wore the glacially cold look that had come Kelly's way when she'd first come to stay at the Hall.

'Hello, Byron.' Elaine spoke first, her eyes fixed on Byron's face as if she too was trying to read his emotions. Then she looked at Kelly, obviously not wanting her there, but saw that Byron still had his arm round her waist. That brought a slightly cynical curl to her lips. 'So it's like that, is it? You certainly don't waste any time.'

'What do you want, Elaine?' Byron asked shortly, his voice harsh and rasping.

'Isn't that obvious?' she countered.

'Hardly—after two years.'

'I tried to see father in hospital, you must know that.' She frowned impatiently. 'Look, can't we talk alone?'

Byron's hand tightened on Kelly's waist. 'I have nothing to hide from Kelly,' he snapped out.

'Maybe not. But *I* don't care to discuss my personal affairs in front of a stranger,' Elaine answered shortly, betraying the first emotion Kelly had seen.

'I'll go.'

She went to move away but Byron pulled her back. 'No, stay.' He frowned at Elaine. 'I want to know why you're here,' he repeated.

Elaine's mouth grew stubbornly silent, so Kelly said, 'She came because of me. She thinks—thought I was trying to take her place with Charles.'

Byron's head jerked up at that as he stared at Elaine. 'So there is still *something* you care about? How did you know about Kelly?' he demanded.

'Someone in the village writes to me regularly, lets me know how father is; what's going on here.'

'So you know all about us,' Byron said grimly. 'And yet you've never once bothered to write and let us know where you were, whether you were all right.'

Elaine looked at him mutely, but there was so much bitterness back in his voice that Kelly couldn't stand it any longer. Twisting out of his hold, she said, 'You don't really want me here. I'll be back at the house.' She waited for a moment, but this time Byron didn't try to stop her, didn't even appear to have heard her as he stood with his eyes fixed on the girl he had once wanted to make his wife.

Turning, Kelly ran out of the yard, but didn't go straight back to the house, instead going into the garden to wait there. She felt torn by anxiety and suddenly completely insecure. She supposed that Elaine would eventually have come home some time, but why did it have to be now, when her relationship with Byron was only really beginning? It was so new, so delicate, still so open to outside influences. And she was worried about Charles, too. He had been so ill, and knowing that Elaine was here might upset him dreadfully. What if he refused to see his own daughter again? Or what if he saw her but it didn't work out and made him ill again? There were so many possibilities, and all of them dangerous.

Kelly found that she felt fiercely protective towards her new relations—Charles almost as much as Byron. She didn't want them to be hurt again. She didn't want their lives disrupted when they had both begun to be so much happier lately. But wasn't that why Elaine had come back: because she'd heard that someone else was making them happy? So exactly what was it that had brought her here? Fear of losing her father's love? But surely she must have felt that she'd forfeited that already? Jealousy? But why be jealous of someone usurping your place when you'd voluntarily walked out of it? Yet something must have brought her back, and it must have been a very strong emotion at that. So—Kelly reluctantly faced a third possibility—had she come back because she'd realised that she was still in love with Byron? Or maybe she wasn't in love with him, but wanted all that he could offer her: this beautiful house that she must still think of as home, the estate, and all the money that went with it. If Elaine had been trying to make a living for herself this last couple of years, she must have missed all the comfort and luxury dreadfully. And the horses and the beautiful countryside. Kelly knew that if she had to leave it now she would certainly miss it, too.

It must have been well over half an hour that she'd been waiting in the garden before Kelly saw Byron coming across from the stables. He walked purposefully, his face set, and made straight for the house. He's going to tell Charles, Kelly guessed.

She moved forward until she was sure that he'd seen her, but he made no move to come to her. For a moment she felt bitterly rejected, but tried hard to be sensible about it, telling herself that his mind must be full of the best way to break the news to Charles without upsetting him. He'll tell me about it later, she comforted herself. The best thing I can do now is to keep out of the way. But that was very hard when someone you loved was so deeply involved.

Remembering that Elaine would be alone, Kelly walked back to the stables and found her standing in front of the stall where Byron's stallion had his head out of the half-open stable door.

Elaine was stroking him casually and Kelly envied her confidence; she was still half afraid of the large, skittish animal.

Elaine looked quickly round when she heard her. 'Has Byron sent you?'

'No.' Kelly shook her head. 'I thought I'd come and keep you company.'

'I'm not going to tell you what happened between Byron and me, if that's what you came to find out,' Elaine said tartly.

Her face tightening, Kelly said shortly, 'It isn't.'

Elaine threw her a look. 'Sorry.' She frowned. 'I'm not sure how to make you out sometimes. Are you in love with Byron?'

'I guess it's my turn to tell you to mind your own business,' Kelly said steadily.

'Which means you are.' Elaine shrugged. 'I don't blame you; he's quite a catch. I'm only surprised he hasn't already married somebody on the rebound.'

'Maybe *he* has more self-control,' Kelly replied pointedly.

Elaine gave the ghost of a smile. 'Meaning that I

should have had more self-control than to run away,
I suppose. Maybe you're right. But if Byron hadn't
gone away when he did, perhaps it would never have
happened.'

'You mean you wouldn't have run away?'

'Perhaps I wouldn't have needed to—perhaps I
might have gone ahead and married him.'

A cold chill ran down Kelly's spine despite the
heat, as if someone had walked over her grave. 'Are
you blaming Byron for what happened, then?' she
demanded belligerently.

In a sudden burst of honesty, Elaine shook her
head and sighed. 'No. It was my fault. But I felt
trapped. I had to get away. And then father had his
accident and wouldn't see me.' She gave Kelly a
sidelong glance. 'Do you know about that?' And,
when Kelly nodded, 'There isn't much you haven't
found out, is there?'

'I'm sorry if you think I ought not to know,' Kelly
answered steadily enough. 'But I've been here for
over two months, I've heard things. And anyway it
isn't exactly a secret, is it?'

'No, it's impossible to have any secrets in
Ashdon,' Elaine declared bitterly.

'But it works both ways, doesn't it. If there hadn't
been gossip about me, you probably wouldn't have
come back now.'

'*Touché*. That's French, by the way. It
means . . .'

'I know what it means,' Kelly interrupted. 'I'm
Canadian—I speak French as well as I do English.'

Elaine gave her an almost wary look. 'I must
remember not to underestimate you, mustn't I?' She
kept giving impatient glances towards the archway
leading from the stables, evidently anxious for Byron

to come back. But suddenly she turned to Kelly and said in an almost fierce tone, 'Just why *did* you come here? What do you want?'

'Why did *you* come back?' Kelly countered. 'What do *you* want?'

Elaine's chin came up. 'I have every right to be here,' she retorted.

'Do you? Are you sure you didn't forfeit that right when you walked out?'

For a moment the two girls faced each other antagonistically, then Elaine gave a smile that was totally disarming. 'Haven't you ever heard of the return of the prodigal?' she said lightly.

The change of mood was so swift that Kelly blinked, and for the first time realised that Elaine had attractions other than the obvious ones of a slim figure and pretty face. She had a natural charm behind the outward reserve; another attribute inherited from her father.

'Elaine.'

Byron's voice from the archway made them both look quickly round. Her shoulders went back as if expecting a blow, and Elaine said, 'Yes?'

Byron walked slowly over, his face set, and Kelly was sure that Charles had again rejected his daughter, but Byron said shortly. 'He's agreed to see you.'

That 'agreed' revealed a lot: why he had been so long, and the fact that he must have put up an argument on Elaine's behalf. A thought that hurt Kelly, even though she tried not to let it.

'But he insists that I'm there, too,' Byron was going on. 'I'm sorry, but he stipulated that condition. He feels that you owe me an explanation, and until that's made it will be impossible to go forward.'

'If I know him, Father will also expect me to make you an abject apology,' Elaine said wryly.

'Probably, but it need hardly concern you.' The edge of bitterness was back in his voice, and both girls noticed it. Two pairs of eyes, one grey, the other brown, searched his face, but neither learnt anything from it. 'Perhaps it's just as well he insisted,' Byron added. 'If you've heard all the local gossip, then you'll know that he was ill again some weeks ago. I don't want him upset by this interview any more than is necessary. If I think it's getting too much for him I shall put an end to it. Do you understand, Elaine?'

'Yes, all right.' She strode forward. 'Why don't we go and get it over with?' And she caught his arm so that he turned and began to walk along with her as she hurried towards the house.

As Kelly watched them turn out of the stableyard, Elaine's hand still familiarly on Byron's arm, she felt terribly bereft, as if something she loved had been torn from her. She tried to tell herself that it was only right and natural that Byron should argue on Elaine's behalf with Charles. And it was good that he was going to be there to protect Charles, to stop father and daughter from emotionally tearing at each other when Charles was so physically weak. But it didn't help, Kelly felt very much the stranger and outsider that, in reality, she was. What was a couple of months and a relationship that had only just been declared beside the years that Byron and Elaine had shared and a love that had grown with those years? OK, Elaine had dealt it a crippling blow, but if she wanted to take it up again would Byron be able to refuse her? Would he even want to?

Kelly sat down on the bench in the stableyard where Elaine had been sitting, and wondered if today was going to be first the happiest and then the worst day of her life.

Getting rather agitatedly to her feet some time later, Kelly wondered what she was supposed to do. She couldn't just go on sitting here until someone remembered she existed. Possibly it might be wise to absent herself from the house until the reconciliation between Charles and his daughter had taken place. And the reconciliation between Byron and Elaine, too? The thought slipped like a devilish imp into her mind and hung on tenaciously. Desperately she tried to push it aside and be practical. If she wanted to go out she would need money, but her purse was back at the house, and she didn't want to go there in case they saw her and thought she was nosing in on a wholly family matter. But she was family too, wasn't she? Kelly thought resentfully. Not as close as Byron had almost been, though.

In the end she just went for a very long, very energetic walk over the hills and came back at about four in the afternoon, hot, thirsty, and too desperate to know what had happened to stay away any longer. As soon as she reached the garden, she knew. The three of them were sitting out on the lawn, round a table laden with tea things: delicate china, a cake stand and plates of little triangular sandwiches with the crusts cut off. Afternoon tea as only the British could do it. There were only three chairs round the table. And Elaine looked every inch at home, pouring out the tea and smiling at her father, back in her rightful place again with the two men in her life. Only, one of them is mine, Kelly thought fiercely, and I'll be damned if I let her have him!

Deciding that she'd rather not start her battle for Byron in sneakers and a sweat-stained shirt, Kelly circled the house and went in by the kitchen, saying a quick 'Hi' to Mrs Banks before running upstairs to shower and change. She selected a pale cream dress and matching sandals, did her hair and applied what was definitely warpaint, and went down ready for the first skirmish.

Byron got to his feet when he saw her come out into the garden, and moved his chair round for her. 'Hello, Kelly. Come and join us. I looked for you but couldn't find you.'

'No, I've been having a very pleasant day exploring the countryside,' Kelly lied. She glanced quickly at Byron's face, but read no message for her there, so sat down in the chair he held for her. Charles looked tentatively happy, as if he didn't yet dare to believe that Elaine had come home, making Kelly feel a spurt of anger that his happiness should depend on such a slender thread as Elaine's wilfulness.

'Would you like some tea?' Elaine asked, making it absolutely plain that she was back in her position as mistress of the household. 'Or do Americans only drink coffee?'

'I don't know about Americans,' Kelly replied calmly, 'but Canadians certainly drink tea. But just a little milk and no sugar. Thank you.'

'Byron tells me you know all about my daughter,' Charles said. 'I'm glad of that. And glad that she has come to see us. You two should be friends. It will be good for you both to have some female company for a while.'

Kelly smiled dutifully. Charles had said that Elaine had come to *see* him. Did that mean she wasn't here to stay? Was she on sufferance? But he'd also said they would be company for each other for a while. Until which one of them left? she wondered feverishly.

Tea progressed, with Kelly hating every minute of the ritual. She longed to be alone with Byron, to find out what had happened, but even more to be held in his arms and reassured that it was *her* he wanted. She stole glances at him under her lashes and her heart contracted at the frown between his eyes. And he hardly looked at her, his gaze fixed broodingly on Charles or Elaine. There was tension on every side; even Charles, who should have been happy, plucked nervously at the blanket over his legs. Kelly's heart went out to him, and she wondered what reason Elaine had given him for coming home. Conversation flagged and died, and everyone seemed to give an inner sigh of relief when at last the meal was over.

Elaine went inside to unpack her case, and Kelly looked at Byron hopefully, but he had arranged a meeting with one of the tenant farmers who wanted to make some alterations to his house, and went off to his study. Kelly went with Charles to his sanctum but, although he was very well mannered about it, he made it plain that he wanted to be alone. So Kelly didn't see any of them again until dinner, a meal that was, if anything, more difficult than tea had been. They ate in the big dining-room, spaced out along the table, with the two men either end. Elaine did most of the talking, asking about people she knew and so shutting Kelly out. And Elaine must have already known the answers to her own questions if she'd been receiving a report of everything that happened in the village from her friend, Kelly thought cynically. But it pleased Charles that she

was taking such an interest, and towards the end of
the meal he even looked up at the blank space on the
wall and murmured something about replacing
Elaine's portrait some time.

After dinner they went into the drawing-room,
and Elaine forestalled any tentative plans Kelly had
to get Byron alone by saying, 'Father tells me that
you usually have a game of chess with him every
evening, Kelly. Please don't let my being here stop
you. I know he enjoys it so much.'

As Charles immediately agreed, Kelly had no
choice but to smile and accept his challenge, but
wasn't at all surprised when a quarter of an hour or
so later Elaine turned to Byron and suggested a stroll
in the garden. Kelly looked at Byron, her eyes wide
and imploring. He caught her glance and frowned a
little, but after a moment's hesitation got up and
opened the french doors for Elaine to precede him
into the garden. Kelly turned back to the chessboard
but couldn't see it properly because her eyes were
suddenly misty. Oh, hell!   She sniffed rather
defiantly and wondered when *she* was going to get a
chance to be alone with Byron. With her fiancé.
With the man who only this morning had told her he
loved her. That thought gave a degree of comfort,
and her spirits lifted even further when she
remembered that Byron had promised to come to
her tonight. *Then* they would be able to talk this
thing through, to decide on their own future and
how Elaine's return would affect it. And they would
be close, loving. It was natural that Byron should be
preoccupied with Elaine this evening, but tonight he
would be all Kelly's and everything would be all
right again.

This thought so lightened her spirits that when

Byron and Elaine came back to the drawing-room they found Kelly and Charles both laughing delightedly together. Elaine gave them a swift, surprised look and came to place a possessive hand on her father's shoulder. That the gesture was new to him was obvious, because Charles looked quite flustered for a moment. He wasn't the demonstrative type, which rather shut other people out, and he didn't expect it in return.

Kelly looked from Elaine to Byron, wondering what had passed between them. Her eyes met Elaine's briefly and she thought she saw a flash of triumph in the other girl's eyes, but it was too fleeting to be sure. Byron, of course, was at his most inscrutable—and most maddening. There was no chance to talk to him privately that evening, and Kelly could almost have thought that he was trying to avoid being alone with her. But then it occured to her that he, too, was waiting until tonight, and she was happy again. It was such an awkward situation, with everyone's emotions tense and on edge; Byron was far wiser to wait until they had plenty of time and could talk when they wouldn't be interrupted.

The thought of the night to come brought Kelly to her feet. 'I guess I'll say goodnight. That walk today has made me feel tired.'

'Yes, it's been a long day for all of us,' Charles agreed. 'I think I'll turn in, too. Byron, would you mind . . .'

Byron went to help him into his wheelchair, and only said goodnight to Kelly over his shoulder.

'I expect you're tired, too,' Kelly said to Elaine. 'Er—do you have everything you need? I know you didn't bring much with you.'

'Thanks, but I still have a lot of clothes that I left behind here. They haven't been thrown away,' Elaine answered with that amused look back in her eyes.

'Oh, yes, of course.' But Kelly didn't mind the amusement, because soon she would be held close in Byron's arms and Elaine would be the last thing on either of their minds.

Up in her room, Kelly put on her most glamorous nightgown, one that she'd bought in Gloucester, and she looked at her reflection in the mirror for a long moment, trying to see herself through Byron's eyes. She was really nothing like Elaine, but she *was* long-legged and slim and attractive. And Byron wanted her and wanted her body, that at least she was sure of. Kelly smiled to herself, the small, secret smile of a woman who knows she has power over a man. She turned off all the lights except the lamp beside the bed, and found the novel she was reading. As she got into bed she heard Elaine's light step in the corridor outside and then her door closing, just two down from Kelly's own.

Kelly held the book in her hands but didn't attempt to read. She knew that Byron would go to the stables to make a last check on the horses, and so wasn't surprised when it was a good half-hour later before she heard the front door close and the bolts shot across, then, a few minutes later, his tread on the landing. She waited, breathless, for him to come to her room, but his steps went right by. Of course, she thought, blaming her own stupidity, he's gone to his room to shower and change first. But he didn't come. After two hours Kelly ran out of excuses and turned off the light, but she lay very still, staring into the darkness for several hours longer before she at last fell asleep.

CHAPTER EIGHT

GETTING up at seven every morning to go to work had given Kelly an alarm clock in her head, and even the next morning, after such a brief sleep, it woke her again. She turned, still tired, to face the window, but saw the sunlight and was instantly completely awake—and completely unhappy. She didn't know how she was going to face Byron or what she was going to say to him. Last night she had got so mad that she been strongly tempted to march down to his room and demand to know what the hell he was playing at. But a girl had to have *some* pride, for God's sake, and she had somehow stopped herself from making a scene. But now she still had to face him today.

There was no point in trying to go back to sleep. Kelly dressed and went down to the empty kitchen to make herself a cup of coffee. The place suddenly felt oppressive and she went out into the garden and sat on a low wall, her back to the house, while she drank it. The slanting morning sunlight cast long, insubstantial shadows across the lawns, the sky as yet still veiled with haze. It would be hot again later, a perfect English spring day, when flowers would open their delicate petals in worship of the sun, revealing their ephemeral beauty, so perfect and yet so soon gone. It made Kelly feel terribly sad. It made her want to cry. That was all it was, just the beauty of the morning. Because she was darned if she was going to cry over Byron Thorne.

Even as she thought about him, Kelly heard Byron come out of the kitchen door and start to walk across the paving to the path that led to the stables. Then she heard his footsteps hesitate as he must have caught sight of her. She waited, all her senses frozen, until she heard him turn and walk slowly towards her.

'Hello, Kelly.' He stopped a yard or so behind her.

'Hi.' She didn't look round. 'Isn't it a beautiful morning?'

'Are you—all right?'

'Sure. Fine. In fact, I feel like a queen.'

'A queen?' There was amused surprise in Byron's voice and he moved forward to stand beside her.

'That's right. Marie Antoinette. You know, the one who was 'mightily undisturbed' on her wedding night.'

She looked up at him then and wasn't surprised to see his jaw harden. 'Last night was hardly an appropriate time, in the circumstances. I thought you would have realised that.'

'Why? *Our* circumstances were the same, weren't they?'

'Hardly—with Elaine's room so close.'

'You said yesterday that you didn't care who knew about us. You said a lot of other things, too.' Putting down her empty mug, she got to her feet and faced him. 'Or has that changed now?'

Byron frowned and thrust his hands into his pockets, a mannerism Kelly was coming to recognise. 'Basically, no. But seeing Elaine again was a shock. She's so different—and yet so very much the same. And she's vulnerable. She's still very unsure of herself with Charles, and she's going to need a lot of support. And Charles, too. It isn't going to be easy for him, either.'

'So what are you saying?' Kelly demanded, her shoulders unknowingly braced.

'That I think it would be best if we left things as they are for the moment. The situation is complicated enough without our adding to it.'

Kelly's face became very pale as she said, 'And just where are we, Byron? What are we? Are we lovers—or not? Are we engaged—or not?'

Byron gave a rather helpless shake of his head. 'Kelly, I can't even think straight yet. Can't you even begin to imagine what it was like, seeing her again after all this time? It was like being kicked in the brain. To be honest, I don't know how I feel.'

'I see. So—so where does that leave me?'

'I don't know. I'm sorry. I can only ask you to be patient for a while until things sort themselves out a little.'

'Until Elaine makes up her mind what she wants, don't you mean?' Kelly said bitterly.

'Until she and Charles decide whether or not she's going to stay for good, yes. I think they'll both need me for a while. Everything is very on edge at the moment.'

'And what about me?' Kelly said in sudden anger. 'Do you think I don't need you? Do you think I didn't need you last night, even if it was only to say that you . . .' She broke off and her head came up. 'Do you want me to go away?'

'No!' The reply was swift and heartening. 'No, of course not. But I . . .' He sighed, then said, 'Kelly, I wanted you to take time to think things over and be very clear in your mind. Now I want you to do the

same for me. Let me get used to the idea of Elaine
being here, give me time to think straight again. I
think it would be best if we gave each other some
space for a while. Will you do that?'

'If that's what you want.' But she said it sadly,
thinking that really it was only feelings that
mattered, and that if Byron wasn't sure now he
never would be.

'Thanks.' He took his hand from his pocket and
started to reach out to take hers, but glanced up at
the house as he did so and then stopped. 'I'd better
go and see to the horses,' he said abruptly, and
walked away, making no attempt to ask her to go
with him.

Kelly watched him go and then she, too, glanced
back at the house. Elaine was watching from one of
the upper windows. She waved to Kelly and smiled
before turning away.

The next few days were sheer hell, but Kelly lived
through them tenaciously. She had expected most of
the unpleasantness to come from Elaine and had
grimly braced herself to face it, but the other girl,
although withdrawn at first, seemed to slowly thaw
and become a person who in other circumstances
Kelly felt she could like. As Elaine's first nervous-
ness and insecurity began to wear off and she spent
more time with her father, so her need to re-establish
her position in the household lessened. But there
were still flashes of jealousy and her moods were
temperamental, so that, although she might be quite
friendly towards Kelly one minute, the next she was
making it clear that Kelly was only a guest. And yet
Elaine was wise enough to see that Charles enjoyed
Kelly's company, so she made no outright move to
try to drive her away. But she did spend a lot

of time with Byron, and it was this that made Kelly feel the most wretched.

Daisy Pickman was still away, so it became natural for Elaine to go to the stables with Byron both morning and night. And when Kelly was having her usual game of chess with Charles in the evenings, Elaine always suggested a walk round the garden with Byron. And Byron always agreed. That was what hurt the most. Kelly tried to tell herself that it would all work out, and she tried hard to put a brave face on things, but it became increasingly difficult. Byron never suggested that he and Kelly take a walk or go out together, and she began to give up hope that he would. She was very tempted to try and force the issue, but she had promised to give him some time and she would keep that promise as far as she could. But it was very hard, especially when Cousin Charles would glance up at them from the chessboard and look pleased when he saw Byron and Elaine go out into the garden together. He didn't say anything, of course, but it was obvious to Kelly that he still hoped that the two would eventually marry, after all.

There was a small car in the garage that Mrs Banks sometimes used; Kelly had been given permission to use it when she first arrived but she hadn't bothered before. Now she began to go out in it nearly every day, even when Byron was home. She drove all round the area: to Broadway, where a tiny river with hump-backed stone bridges over it ran through the middle of the town, to an old house owned by the National Trust, whose previous owner had collected like a magpie, everything from Japanese Samurai armour to toys and clocks. Every room was full of curiosities, so full that in the

end the collector had moved out into a tiny garden
house to live and had given the big house over to his
beloved mass of artefacts. It fascinated Kelly
too—for a while. And she loved to drive through old
villages, each as lovely as the last, with narrow
streets and churches with towers and tall spires.
There were quaint shops with low, bow-fronted
windows full of goods, red post-boxes with the
initials of long dead kings and queens entwined on
them, and inns with painted signs called the Four in
Hand and the Dog and Duck. It was beautiful, but
she felt so alone.

After over a week of this Kelly suddenly knew that
she couldn't take any more. It came to a head when
she drove home at about five one afternoon and saw
Byron and Elaine together. They had been out
riding and were making their way up the driveway.
Byron on his stallion and Elaine on the hunter. They
were laughing together and looked—looked companionable. Kelly slowed down to go past them, and
it hit her then that she had to do something fast or
she was going to lose Byron.

The weather, as mercurial as it always was in
England, and changed that afternoon. The sky was
heavy and overcast, and the wind was beginning to
blow strongly, whipping the tops of the trees and
tearing the petals from the flowers. The sudden
harshness of the weather matched Kelly's mood as
she got ready for dinner that evening. She realised
that it would have to be now or never, and that
whatever she decided to do would be pretty drastic.
Her first thought was to go to Byron's room tonight
when Elaine was asleep. Byron had said he wanted
her and she could play on that—and if once they
made love again, then he would be hers, she was

sure of that. He would feel himself committed.

But wasn't that taking a rather underhand
advantage? And what if he sent her away, rebuffed
her? Kelly had read that people lost their pride when
they were in love, but she clung to hers, hurt as it
already was. If she had to walk out of this, then she
wanted to go with some kind of dignity still left.
Even if she fell to pieces afterwards, she wanted to
leave with her head held high.

So that left only one thing that might work. She
would have to tell Byron that the position he had put
her in was intolerable and that he had to make up his
mind or she would leave. And she had to mean it.
Kelly was quite sure that Byron would see straight
through any pretence and think the worse of her for
it. Not that there *was* any pretence, because she
couldn't take any more. But she couldn't afford to
wait, because then she would have time to realise
that if this didn't work she would never see him
again. Her heart growing desolate at the thought,
Kelly decided that she would demand to speak to
him alone, immediately after dinner.

The decision gave her courage and she dressed
quickly, already on tenterhooks. She was too early,
there was nearly an hour to wait yet. Rather than go
down, Kelly turned on the radio beside her bed to
hear the news, and then froze as the announcer
began with the day and the date. Oh, hell! Kelly had
forgotten that this was Tuesday. Because every
alternate Tuesday Byron had to go to some sort of
business cum social dinner with the local Rotary
Club, and this was the day to go. Which meant that
she wouldn't be able to speak to him unless she
waited until he came home, which often wasn't until
gone midnight.

To wait that long was unbearable. Without stopping to think, Kelly ran along the corridor to Byron's room and rapped on the door.

'Who is it?' Byron's muffled voice came from the other side.

'Kelly.'

There was an interminable pause, and for a few dreadful moments she thought that he was going to ignore her, but then Byron opened the door. His eyes went swiftly to her face and read the determination there, the words he was about to speak dying on his lips.

Kelly walked past him into the room and closed the door firmly behind her. 'I have to talk to you,' she said tonelessly.

Byron slowly moved from the door towards her. He was wearing trousers and had on a shirt over his bare chest, but it was still unbuttoned, the cuffs undone. Kelly looked at the dark mat of hairs on his chest and gulped, remembering that night on the rug before the fire. She tried to push the memory aside, tried to be firm and strong, but she longed to run into his arms, to be held and kissed and loved. She tried to speak but couldn't, the silence becoming tense and brittle.

'What is it, Kelly?' Byron broke it, his voice cold and withdrawn.

'I think you know.' Somehow she managed to lift her chin and face him.

'I thought we'd agreed that I needed some time to . . .'

'You've had plenty of time,' she interrupted him. 'All you're doing is putting off making a decision. And that isn't fair. It's—it's cruel, Byron.'

'I'm sorry if you think that. But it isn't so.'

He ran a harassed hand through his hair. 'Look, this is hardly the time to talk this through. You know that I'm going out this evening and I really must finish dressing.'

'So be late for once,' Kelly said shortly. 'This is important and it has to be settled *now*.' Her voice broke and she had to bite her lip hard. 'You either— you either love me or you don't. You either meant what you said and you still want to marry me—or not. Which is it, Byron?'

His jaw tightened. 'And what if I'm not ready to make that decision?'

Kelly's heart contracted, and it was very hard to even speak, let alone keep her voice steady as she said, 'I've already said that I can't stand being in this ambiguous position any longer. If you won't—won't decide, then I guess I'll just have to leave.'

'I see.' His jaw thrust forward as Byron glared at her grimly. 'So you've decided to force my hand. I don't know what they call that in Canada, but here it's known as moral blackmail.'

'It is *not*!' Bright flashes of anger rose on Kelly's pale cheeks. 'I have a *right* to do this. *You* gave me that right when you asked me to marry you. Damn you, Byron, I'm not even sure that I want to be in love with you any more.' She put an agitated hand up to her mouth and bit her knuckles, then dashed it away as she said furiously, 'Do you think I wanted to fall in love with you? Well, I didn't. I wanted to go back home and meet some nice ordinary man and lead an ordinary life in a city apartment and have a cabin in the mountains for holidays. And instead of that I had to come here and meet *you*. A cold, reserved Englishman who doesn't even know his own heart.'

'And maybe you don't, either,' Byron hit back curtly, a flame of anger in his own eyes. 'You're threatening to leave and yet you were the one who said you'd always be here, that you'd never walk out on me. So maybe I'm beginning to see just how much your promises are worth.'

Kelly stared at him aghast, only now seeing the pitfall she'd blundered into. 'It isn't like that,' she said desperately, and went forward to catch his wrist. 'You know I love you. You know I want to stay. But how can I when you treat me like this?' She looked up at him imploringly and put her hand on his chest, trying to convey how she felt.

'You're just like Elaine—too young to know your own mind. I should never have let myself fall for you. I was a fool to even hope that we could make a future together. And now you've proved it.'

'No, that isn't true.' Kelly let go of his wrist and put her arms round him under his shirt, her own arms bare against his skin.

Byron put his hands on her shoulders with an angry exclamation and went to push her away. But then his fingers tightened compulsively, digging into her flesh, and suddenly his mouth was on hers, kissing her with a savage, undeniable hunger. Kelly gave a gasping moan and returned it avidly. Her hands went up to his head as she opened her mouth under his fierce, demanding lips. She muttered words under his mouth, forceful words of love and longing that were merely sounds beneath his own frenzied need as passion increased and he bent her against him, crushing her unresisting body against his.

It lasted only a few moments, that fierce,

shatteringly urgent embrace, and then it was over as
suddenly as it began. Byron made a violent
movement and stepped away from her, so suddenly
that Kelly almost fell. 'Dear God!' he swore.
'Did you have to try and blackmail me that way,
too?'

Kelly recovered herself and stared at him, her
breathing still ragged. Then she straightened and
said with painful dignity, 'If you can call that
blackmail and not love, then I don't think there's
any hope left for us.' She waited for him to deny it,
but Byron stood silently, his face taut, a smouldering
glint of anger in his eyes. 'I shall leave tomorrow,'
Kelly said shortly. 'And I shall be glad to go.
Because you're a coward, Byron, and I don't want
anything to do with a man who's afraid to trust his
own feelings.'

Somehow she got out of his room and back down
the corridor to her own. She went in, shut the door
and locked it. And only then did her trembling limbs
collapse so that she sank to the floor and put her
head in her hands, rocking her body backwards and
forwards in silent pain, her despair and anguish too
deep to cry.

She lay on the floor a long time, hearing Byron's
footsteps stride by and later Elaine's as she went
down to dinner. But after a while Elaine came back
again and knocked on her door. 'Kelly, are you
coming down to dinner? We're waiting for you.'

Kelly would have given everything she possessed
to say no and stay in the sanctuary of her own room,
but stubborn pride made her call out unsteadily,
'What?' Oh, sure. Sorry, I forgot the time. I'll be
right down.'

Going to the mirror, Kelly brushed her hair,

trying not to look at her eyes and see the haunting misery there. At least there were no tears to try to hide, and for that she was thankful. But she knew that the tears would come later, when there was no one to see.

In some ways dinner was easier because Byron wasn't there. She managed to tell Charles where she'd been that day when he asked, and listened with apparent attentiveness when he gave her a potted history of the place. He talked, too, about taking her and Elaine to see an old ruined monastery the next day. Should I tell him now that I'm going? Kelly wondered. Perhaps she ought to have done, but her mind shrank from the questions they were bound to ask and even more from the evasive answers she would have to try and give, and which Elaine at least was bound to see through. So she somehow creased her face into a smile and said that it sounded great.

She had to raise her voice to say it, the wind had got so loud, howling round the old house and through the branches of the many surrounding trees, most of them having the new leaves torn from them even before they had their full foliage. There was a crash from outside as they were eating dessert, and Charles frowned in worry. 'I wonder what that was. Ask Jim Banks to go and have a look, will you, Elaine?'

'I think they've already left. If you remember, they were going to that whist drive in the village tonight to raise funds for the church hall. But I'll go and have a look in a minute.'

When they'd finished eating, Elaine collected up the dishes and Kelly followed her into the kitchen to make the coffee.

'It was a tile from the roof of the garage,' Elaine reported when she came back, a torch in her hand. 'It blew off and hit the wall of the house.'

'Is it still raining?'

'Absolutely sleeting down. And the wind is fiercer than ever. I think it's the worst gale I've ever seen.'

They went back to the drawing-room, and Kelly sat down to play her usual game of chess with Charles, but the storm grew so bad that it buffeted against the windows, making the panes rattle, and even the house, as old and solid as it was, seemed to shake on its foundations.

After a while of increasing uneasiness, Elaine stood up and said, 'I think I'll go and check on the horses.'

'You mustn't go alone,' Charles intervened at once. 'Wait until Byron or Jim Banks get back.'

'They could be hours. I really ought to go.'

'It's all right. I'll go with her,' Kelly offered.

Charles didn't like that idea much, either, but he was worried about the horses too, and there was no other choice. So the two girls dressed themselves in wellington boots, macs and rainhats, and, armed with the torch, set off for the stables.

As soon as they stepped out of the door, the howling wind caught at them and almost knocked them over. Kelly clung to the porch and felt the rainhat whipped from her head. 'Are you OK?' she yelled at Elaine.

The other girl nodded and they set out, holding on to each other as they battled their way through the storm. It was blowing against them and each step was a physical effort. And it was so noisy; Kelly would never have believed that wind could howl so loudly. But even through that terrible din they heard the greater noise of a tall fir tree, torn up by its fragile roots and sent crashing to the ground. Kelly heard it happen, but strangely wasn't afraid—but then she had never been afraid of storms; their wild primevalness appealed to something in her nature and filled her with a strange fascination and excitement.

But Elaine gave a gasp of fear and flinched away. Kelly looked at her face through the driving rain and saw that she was terrified. 'Go back,' she yelled. 'I'll see to them.'

Elaine shook her head stubbornly. 'No. I know how to handle them.'

They went on, saving their breath for the battle against the storm, but Kelly now had a protective arm around Elaine and took the torch from her because her hands were shaking too much to hold it. They reached the stables at last, and, although it was only a couple of hundred yards, to Kelly it seemed the longest journey she had ever made. It was a blessed relief to go inside out of the wind, but this building wasn't as solid as the house and even in here the noise was terribly loud. The horses were all jumpy and restless, neighing nervously, and the stallion was kicking at the door of his stall.

Elaine lost her fear immediately she went inside and began to go to each in turn, soothing them and making sure they hadn't injured themselves. When she got to the stallion's stall it took her longer to quieten him and then she said worriedly, 'He's gashed his leg on the door and there's a big splinter in the wound. I'll have to try and take it out.'

Kelly looked at the large animal, but said bravely,

'Can I help?'

'If you could get me the things I need from the tack-room. I don't want to leave him.'

So Kelly went out again and across the stableyard to get the things Elaine had listed, and as she passed the archway between the buildings looked through at the big old oak tree that stood just a few yards behind the stalls. It was groaning under the force of the wind, its gnarled branches swaying and bending as if in some terrible ritual dance of death. Even the earth round its roots moved to the convulsive rhythm.

For a few paralysing seconds Kelly stood frozen with shock, but then her eyes followed the line of the tree and she realised it would come straight down on to the stables with Elaine and the horses inside! Her limbs suddenly finding strength to move again, she turned and raced back to the stable. 'Get them out,' she screamed at Elaine. 'The tree's coming down!'

Elaine turned to stare at her—but didn't move! With a sob, Kelly flung herself at the door of the nearest stall where the mare and her foal were tethered to prevent them injuring themselves, and with shaking hands untied the ropes and ran with them out of the stables and turned them loose, yelling at them so that they ran away. She ran back and saw with relief that Elaine was struggling to get the stallion out, but the highly bred animal was nervous and didn't want to go. Kelly ran to the other mare and got her out and went back for the hunter, while Elaine still struggled with Byron's stallion. But the stallion's nervous neighing and kicking had upset the hunter, and Kelly had a terrible time getting him out. Kelly was equally afraid of him, but he kicked her leg, which made her mad and gave her strength and the will-power to haul him outside. As she set him loose, the groaning of the old tree was shrill and terrible as it fought its last battle against the elements it had withstood for two hundred years. Kelly's ears were torn by the noise, but it never occured to her not to go back and help Elaine.

The stallion had been in the farthest stall. Elaine had got him out into the corridor and half-way along, but the brute was fighting her every step of the way.

'Come on,' Kelly yelled desperately.

'He's terrified,' Elaine screamed back, her voice raw with fear. 'And he won't put his weight on his injured leg.'

Reaching up, Kelly caught the horse's bridle to add her weight to Elaine's, but the stallion reared up and she was sent flying. Then the panic-stricken animal backed into one of the empty stalls and stood there, feet apart, head down, defying them with his far greater strength.

'We'll have to leave him,' Kelly shouted, and dragged herself to her feet. The tree was screaming now, she could hear it, and her heart filled with fear. 'Come on. Get out.'

'No! We've got to get him out first.'

Elaine rushed into the stall and tried to grab the stallion's bridle again. Desperately Kelly went after her, caught hold of her arm and tried to pull her away. But Elaine resisted her and for a few moments they fought together. Then came the most horrific rending noise and the lights went out. Kelly felt the terrible vibration of the earth as much as heard the noise as the great tree was torn from its last hold on the earth and came crashing down on to the stables. Kelly pushed Elaine down into the corner and threw herself down on top of her as the whole place seemed to disintegrate around them. The stallion screamed in terror and ran out into the night as the branches of the huge great tree tore through the roof and the walls like matchwood and came down on top of them.

It seemed a lifetime before the noise and movement stopped, but even then Kelly could hear a terrified moaning in the sudden stillness.

'Elaine? Are you alright?'

But the other girl just went on sobbing in wild, uncontrolled fear.

'Are you hurt? Please stop crying and tell me if you're hurt?'

Kelly tried to move, but her legs were restricted by a branch, although they weren't hurt at all. The two of them were wedged into the angle of the wall, and it was this that had saved them from serious injury, she realised. But they were covered by smaller branches and foliage, as well as fallen masonry, and it was impossible to move. But Kelly could feel Elaine below her and she managed to touch and pat her with her right hand, giving what comfort she could and murmuring words of encouragement until Elaine stopped crying.

And then there was nothing to do but wait for help to come. At first they got very wet, but then the rain stopped and there was only the wind to listen to and the sound of other great trees that lost the battle and fell to the ground, sending shock-waves vibrating through the earth. Kelly was worried about Charles, alone in the house, especially if the electricity had gone there too. She could only hope that Jim and

Enid Banks would hear the storm and come home early.

'Do you think they'll be long?' Elaine mumbled, her voice muffled against her arm.

'No. I'm sure your father would have phoned for help when the lights went out. Someone will soon come.'

They were silent for a while and then Elaine said, 'Kelly, I have to apologise to you. Byron told me he'd asked you to marry him, but I—I asked him not to tell anyone. To wait until everything was all right between Father and me again.'

Kelly had stiffened, but then she said, 'It's all right. It doesn't matter now.' But she couldn't help asking, 'Are you still in love with him?'

'No. But I—well, I told him I wasn't sure. I'm sorry,' she said again. 'But I needed to be sure I still had a place here.' Elaine coughed as some dust from the wall got up her throat. 'I never really was. I was very fond of him and I thought I loved him, but then I realised I wasn't. But he wasn't here to tell so I ran away.'

'But he was in love with you,' Kelly stated.

'Yes, he was.'

'And now?' Kelly waited for Elaine to answer, but thought she saw a flash of light through the dense bulk of the branches around them. It became stronger and she realised that it was the headlights of a car. 'They've come,' she said urgently. 'There's someone here.'

There was a brief lull in the storm, and she heard shouts and then footsteps running across the stable-yard towards them. 'Kelly?' It was Byron's voice, but as she'd never heard it before, raw with fear. 'Oh, my God, no!' she heard as he came nearer and saw how much damage the tree had done. 'Kelly!' His voice grew desperate. 'Kelly! For God's sake, answer me.'

She tried, but there was this great lump of emotion in her throat and she couldn't speak. So it was Elaine who cried out, 'Byron, we're here. Over by the wall.'

'I'm coming.' They heard him scrambling over the broken branches and a torch probed the darkness. 'Elaine, is Kelly with you? Is she all right?' His voice was brittle with urgency and fear.

And then the torch was on her, revealing the way she'd covered the other girl. Kelly blinked back silly tears and managed to smile and wiggle her hand. 'Hi,' she said huskily.

'Oh, thank God!' The relief in his voice was enormous. Somehow he managed to weave his arm through the branches until their hands touched. Kelly held on to his very tightly for a long moment, their joined hands conveying a million messages that they couldn't say. But then there was another shout and Byron said raggedly, 'Don't worry, we'll soon have you out of here.' And then he was gone, climbing back to direct the men who had come to help.

It took a long time to get them out. There were firemen there and policemen too, all doing their best, but there were trees down across the roads and the driveway, and they had to manhandle the chain-saws and lifting tackle to cut through the branches and lift them out of the way.

But at last the branches that restricted her legs were cut away and Kelly was able to squirm round and reach up to be lifted out. A strong pair of arms took hold of her, and she knew even before he spoke that it was Byron.

'Are you sure you're not hurt?' he demanded as soon as he'd lifted her clear.

'No, only bruised and battered. Oh, Byron!' Her arms went round his neck and she clung to him as he carried her away from the debris of the stables.

She would have given anything to be alone with him then, but an ambulanceman came hurrying up to wrap her in a blanket and she had a battle to convince him that she wasn't hurt, wasn't in shock, and didn't want to go to hospital. He seemed quite upset at her refusal, quite convinced that she couldn't possibly have been buried under a tree without being hurt. But then they pulled Elaine out and he went off with Byron to see to her.

'Is she all right?' Kelly asked anxiously as Byron came back.

'I think so, but her ankle was badly twisted. They're taking her to hospital to have it X-rayed. Mrs Banks is going with her.' Putting his arm round her, he said, 'Let's get you back to the house. You're soaking.'

'No, I'm OK. And I want to thank everyone first.' And she went round and shook hands with each man that had worked so hard to get them free.

Byron drove her back to the house and she said she ought to go and see Charles. 'He must be terribly worried about Elaine.'

'No, he's followed her to the hospital,' Byron told her. 'Jim Banks took him. And they're all going to stay in Gloucester to be near the hospital until tomorrow.' He turned her to face him. 'So we have the house to ourselves.'

There was something in his voice that made Kelly catch her breath. She turned to him and gave a prayer of thankfulness as she saw the love and tenderness in his eyes. Picking her up, Byron carried her up to her bathroom, stripped off her clothes, and very gently bathed her bruised body. His face darkened when he saw the marks on her, and he bent suddenly to kiss her, both of them aware of how close she had come to being killed. But his touch was infinitely light as he dried her and helped her to put on her nightdress, then put her in the bed.

'Byron.' She caught his hand as he went to turn away. 'You'll stay?' she said urgently.

He smiled. 'Of course.' And kissed her. 'Be back in a few minutes.'

He had showered and put on a robe over pyjama trousers and made her a hot milk drink when he came back.

Kelly smiled. 'It's too late for bedtime drinks.'

'Do as you're told and drink it,' he commanded. 'You were lying there in wet clothes for hours, and I don't want you getting pneumonia.'

She pulled a face at him but secretly loved it. And she was happier still when he got into bed beside her and put his arm round her. He stroked her hair back from her forehead and said slowly, 'I have so much to say to you, I hardly know where to begin—or how,' he added on a note of bitter self-reproach.

'Does it matter—now?' she asked gently.

'I think it does.' He took her hand in his and held it, looking at her fingers as he stroked them. 'You see, after Elaine left, I felt very bitter. And when you came along I didn't even want to fall in love with you. In fact, I tried hard not to. Because I knew that with you it could never be just a passing romance. I think I knew that right from the start. And that made me afraid.'

'Afraid of being hurt again?'

'Yes. And of committing myself, I suppose. Of laying myself open to even the possibility of it not working out. But I wanted you badly, and that night—well, you know what happened that night—I couldn't go on resisting wanting you any longer.'

'But you tried to tell yourself it wasn't love,' Kelly prompted.

Byron grinned. 'I frightened the life out of myself that night, I never thought I'd want someone so badly that I'd lose all my common sense. But when I took you like that . . .' He shook his head at the memory. 'I knew then that I was in love with you, I think, but I was afraid to accept it. So, yes, I tried to reduce it to sexual attraction.' He turned and smiled at her. 'You're not drinking your milk.'

She did so quickly and licked the froth from her lips with the tip of her tongue. Byron watched her and his eyes darkened. 'It definitely *was* sexual chemistry,' he said thickly, 'and a whole lot more besides. I tried to hold off, to get used to the idea, to convince myself that it could work, even though you were from a different background.'

'And you did,' Kelly said softly. 'You asked me to marry you.'

'Yes.' His face shadowed. 'But then Elaine came back.' He paused and said with difficulty, 'It's not going to be easy for you to understand; I'm not even sure if I understand myself. She asked for my help. She said that all she'd wanted by running away was to gain time, and that if I'd been at home she would probably never have gone. I told her about us and she begged me not to say anything to Charles as it would only upset him even more at such an emotional time. I knew that wasn't fair on you, but I felt I had no choice. And then Elaine started saying that she wished she'd never gone away, that we'd gone through with the wedding.'

'That she was still in love with you,' Kelly added.

He gave a sharp look. 'Yes, she said that too. I felt as if I was being torn in half,' he went on. 'Torn between the old love and the new. And with you I was still afraid that it might not work. But somehow it seemed that I owed it to Elaine.'

'Even though she'd walked out on you?' Kelly exclaimed.

'In some confused way, yes. Because I've always felt that I must have unknowingly coerced her into it before she was ready. I think the bitterness was guilt as much as anything. And I was afraid, too, that my making love to *you* was a form of coercion.'

'Oh, Byron,' Kelly put down her mug on the bedside-table and turned to him. 'You certainly were mixed up.'

'Mm.' He held her closer. 'But everything became crystal clear when I got to the house tonight and found that you were both missing. There was only one name that came into my mind. Only one person I knew I couldn't live without.'

He kissed her and Kelly clung to him, unashamed tears on her cheeks. 'Supposing I'd left,' she said in remembered distress.

Byron smiled and bent to kiss away a teardrop. 'I

somehow think it would have given me the kick in the teeth I needed and I'd have been on the first plane after you.'

She smiled, liking the idea, but said, 'What are you going to do about Elaine?'

'Let her stand on her own two feet and sort herself out with Charles. She'd always hoped that he would eventually come round and let her come home, but when she heard about you she was afraid she was going to be cut off for ever, and that's why she came back. But she'll be OK, I think. Charles was terribly worried about her tonight.'

'And us?' she questioned.

'We,' Byron said very definitely, 'are going to get married and take a house in the village so that I can still manage the estate until Charles is good and ready to leave here. But I want you all to myself without anyone else around.'

'Sure, I know, so you can make love to me in front of the fire again,' Kelly said with an unsteady catch in her breath.

'And a great many other places, too,' he agreed. 'But that we'll discuss some other time, because you, my dearest love, have had quite a night. So now I'm going to turn out the light and I'm just going to hold you so that you can sleep it all away. OK? Come on, lie down.'

She obeyed him, easing herself down in the bed. Byron switched off the lamp and lay down beside her, taking her in his arms and holding her snuggled close against him. For a while there was silence in the room, but then Byron said warningly, 'Kelly, stop that. Go to sleep.' But a few moments later he caught his breath and said, 'God, you Canadian girls are really something else.'

Kelly chuckled softly, but then gave a great gasp. 'Oh, wow! And so are Englishmen!'

Harlequin Presents

Coming Next Month

Available in February wherever paperback books are sold, or through Harlequin Reader Service:

In the U.S.
901 Fuhrmann Blvd.
P.O. Box 1397
Buffalo, N.Y. 14240-1397

In Canada
P.O. Box 603
Fort Erie, Ontario
L2A 5X3

A compelling novel of deadly revenge and passion
from Harlequin's bestselling international
romance author Penny Jordan

POWER PLAY

Eleven years had passed but the
terror of that night was something
Pepper Minesse would never
forget. Fueled by revenge against
the four men who had brutally
shattered her past, she set in
motion a deadly plan to destroy
their futures.

Available in February!

 Harlequin Books•

HPP-1A

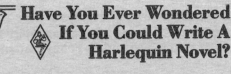

Have You Ever Wondered If You Could Write A Harlequin Novel?

Here's great news—Harlequin is offering a series of cassette tapes to help you do just that. Written by Harlequin editors, these tapes give practical advice on how to make your characters—and your story—come alive. There's a tape for each contemporary romance series Harlequin publishes.

Mail order only

All sales final

TO: **Harlequin Reader Service**
Audiocassette Tape Offer
P.O. Box 1396
Buffalo, NY   14269-1396

I enclose a check/money order payable to HARLEQUIN READER SERVICE® for $9.70 ($8.95 plus 75¢ postage and handling) for EACH tape ordered for the total sum of $_____*
Please send:

☐ Romance and Presents   ☐ Intrigue
☐ American Romance   ☐ Temptation
☐ Superromance   ☐ All five tapes ($38.80 total)

Signature_____
                                        (please print clearly)
Name:_____
Address:_____
State:_____Zip:_____

*Iowa and New York residents add appropriate sales tax.   AUDIO-H

HARLEQUIN Temptation

The Pirate
JAYNE ANN KRENTZ

At the heart of every powerful romance story lies a legend. There are many romantic legends and countless modern variations on them, but they all have one thing in common: They are tales of brave, resourceful women who must gentle and tame the powerful, passionate men who are their true mates.

The enormous appeal of Jayne Ann Krentz lies in her ability to create modern-day versions of these classic romantic myths, and her LADIES AND LEGENDS trilogy showcases this talent. Believing that a storyteller who can bring legends to life deserves special attention, Harlequin has chosen the first book of the trilogy—THE PIRATE—to receive our Award of Excellence. Look for it in February.

AE-PIR-1

Harlequin Superromance®

LET THE GOOD TIMES ROLL . . .

Add some Cajun spice to liven up your New Year's
celebrations and join Superromance for a romantic
tour of the rich Acadian marshlands and the legendary
Louisiana bayous.

Starting in January 1990, we're launching CAJUN
MELODIES, a three-book tribute to the fun-loving
people who've enriched America by introducing us to
crawfish étouffé and gumbo, zydeco music and the
Saturday night party, the *fais-dodo*. And learn about
loving, Cajun-style, as you meet the tall, dark,
handsome men who win their ladies' hearts with a
beautiful, haunting melody. . . .

Book One: *Julianne's Song*, January 1990
Book Two: *Catherine's Song*, February 1990
Book Three: *Jessica's Song*, March 1990

SRCJ-1R